HILLDALE FAREWELL

written by
Pat Jaeger

Grand Circle Publishing, LLC

Hilldale Farewell

Grand Circle Publishing, LLC
Portales NM 88130
Cover design by Joshua Baird © Grand Circle Publishing, LLC all rights reserved. Published in the United States of America.

Christian Fiction/Suspense/Romance

Dedication

To Pastor John Rose who not only brings the reality of the gospel alive, but lives the love of Christ. Pastor John, thank you for all you've given, for all the prayers and compassion for those who cross your path, and for all the sacrifices you've made to bring the love of Jesus to those who are willing to receive it. God bless you.

Hilldale Farewell

Pat Jaeger

"…and provide for those who grieve in Zion—to bestow on them a crown of beauty instead of ashes, the oil of joy instead of mourning, and a garment of praise instead of a spirit of despair. They will be called oaks of righteousness, a planting of the LORD for the display of His splendor."
Isaiah 61:3 NIV

What's Gone On Before

Storm Over Hilldale, Book One of the Hilldale Missouri series, introduces the reader to Sheriff Daniel Halloran, his octogenarian friends, Muley Burger, Kickapoo Billy Sumday, and Obed Martin, who help and hinder him in solving the mystery of the disappearance of Neva Sue Bently.

We meet Gordie Adam Bently, severely abused, and hidden away for the first seventeen years of his life. Two years later, gentle-hearted Gordie becomes a main character in **Home to Hilldale,** Book Two of the Hilldale Missouri series, where we meet a runaway teen, Juanita IraLilly Edmonds.

Gordie steps in to help Sheriff Dan and the town of Hilldale save the young woman's life from the man who tracks her down across state lines, kidnapping her with the intent on forcing her to become his wife.

Juanita finds her grandmother and aunt, and believes her nightmare life has finally turned around for the better. Gordie and the folks of Hilldale rally around Juanita to give this seemingly lost teen the home and family she's always longed for. But will the kidnapper, Eddie Felton, crush her dreams and destroy all the progress Juanita's made in turning her life around? Answers are found in Book Two.

Home to Hilldale finds Sheriff Dan married, and we lose one of our beloved octogenarians. Juanita has a child and we find out if the baby survives the evil intent of Eddie Felton.

Hilldale Farewell, Book Three in the Hilldale Missouri series, begins seven years later. James Baytree is back, and revenge rules his heart and mind. Sheriff Dan Halloran and the folks of Hilldale, Missouri are under siege, suffering losses that will challenge their faith, and forever change them.

PROLOGUE

Water trickled past his face. Rain pummeled his broken body chilling him, even though the morning temperature rose above eighty degrees.

Struggling to raise his head, to keep his nose and mouth clear of the rushing stream, he tried pushing himself up, tried crawling out of the muddy, weed-infested ditch. No good. His legs wouldn't respond, his right arm refused to move. Desperation clawed at him.

Using his left arm, with one last fierce effort, he dragged himself up the side of the ditch. The intense effort brought a fiery agony that raced through his battered body. His scream was dampened by the rain-soaked August morning. Just before darkness claimed him, he got his head cradled on a clump of fox-tail grass, safely out of the rising stream.

Near-by, his fallen horse struggled to her feet. The bullet holes in the paint mare's heaving side and shoulder leaked blood that ran in rivulets, following the paths of old scars. Her eyes rolled, wide with fear.

She staggered over to the man lying so still. Her ears flattened and nostrils flared as she lifted her head and a shrill, pain-filled cry rose to the sky. Trembling, the mare stood over her beloved friend and master, nosing him gently, blowing softly against his muddied face, his twisted, broken body. Stepping carefully, she moved closer, shifting her weight, easing it from her wounded side.

Her fear and pain compelled her to flee, but her love for the wounded man defied her instinct, and with head hanging low, she stood over him, waiting. She would not leave him to die alone.

ONE

Carmen Fuentes stood next to the man she'd been ordered by the court to defend. Nasty, filled-with arrogance, and bitterness, James Baytree looked up at the tall slender woman and hissed threats of what would happen to her if he didn't win his appeal.

Shaking her head, his public defender motioned for him to acknowledge the judge. Her dark toffee brown eyes grew darker with disapproval.

"James Keith Baytree, do you understand the denial of your appeal?" Judge Emmett Anderson stared down at the angry man before him. "You are remanded back into the custody of Missouri Department of Corrections to serve the rest of your sentence—three years, two months, and seventeen days."

With that pronouncement, Judge Anderson whacked his gavel down, sealing Baytree's fate. Fury flashed across the prisoner's face and shot out through his body. He whirled around and grabbed Carmen Fuentes, putting her in a choke-hold, pulling her tight against him.

The courtroom erupted in chaos as Baytree screamed at the bailiff to back off or he'd snap Fuentes' neck. A pathway opened along the aisle and James Baytree pushed the lawyer ahead of him, the two crab-walking out the courthouse door.

The earlier rain storm had passed, leaving the August morning hot and humid, with steam-fairies rising from the pavement. A beat-up Ford F-150 screeched to a stop at the foot of the courthouse steps, the passenger door flying open.

"Hurry up, Pa, I've been around this square so many times folks've noticed. Come on!" Macon Baytree yelled. "Cops are gonna be right behind me."

He revved the souped-up engine and the deep powerful growl that rumbled forth, sent shivers through the woman being pushed into the cab of the truck.

"You're dead meat, mister," her voice trembled with fear and fury. "I don't care if they shoot me, long as they take you and your disgusting son out."

A sharp slap across the side of her head silenced her. She winced at the bruising yank on her arm as the younger Baytree pulled her to the middle of the truck seat. Fear gripped her, glacier cold, causing her to shiver. A pistol lay in his lap. Taking a deep breath, she thrust her hand out. A vice-like grip grabbed and twisted her wrist forcing a pained cry from her.

"Try that again, and I'll break it," Macon snarled, glaring at her. He stomped on the accelerator as his father slid across the seat, pushing hard against Carmen.

Hilldale Farewell

The vehicle skidded away from the curb, the passenger door swinging wildly, tires burning rubber until they gained purchase on the still-damp asphalt. Roaring down the one-way street past the fountain cascading its sparkling water, the truck circled Hilldale's town square. James Baytree yanked the door closed.

"Head to the hide-out, boy, but first drive west. Make 'em think we're headed for the farm. Use the gravel road through the bottoms to get back east. Don't nobody know about your great-grandpa's place."

Poking Carmen in the side, he leered at her. "'Sides, we got our insurance right here, don't we sweetheart."

His cackle filled her with dread. He grasped her knee squeezing hard, the rough caress ripping her panty hose, making her recoil. Grinning at her fear, he reached up and pulled the tortoise shell comb from her hair. Raven black, fragrant waves cascaded around her. Baytree ran a lock through his fingers, holding it to his nose breathing deeply. His eyes glittered. Carmen shuddered.

Dropping the thick strand of hair, he leaned forward. "You take care of that business like I told you, boy?" Baytree looked across Carmen to his son, his expression turning hard.

Macon grinned at his Pa hoping to win his approval. "He ain't going nowhere but the morgue. Horse liked to kick me to death, though. Tried to shoot it, not too sure I hit her. She was crazy wild. She's still running loose." He glanced at his father, his grimy hands tapping the steering wheel, his eyelid twitching. His tongue darted across his lips. Looking back at the road, he continued.

"Whooped that old man good, just like you said. 'Make 'em suffer 'fore he dies.' You ain't mad I didn't get the mare?" The boy gulped, swallowing hard.

James grunted. "Never mind about the horse. I got ways of finding out where she got off to. Good job, boy. Made that Injun suffer, I'm happy.

"'Sides, that mare always did have a mean streak. Tried to beat it out of her, but she's just mean to the bone.

"Long as you took care of the old man, we're good. Teach him to mess with my property." He leered at Carmen. "Privileged information, right?" He laughed, but his eyes were cold steel.

Boone/Lund County Missouri Public Defender, Carmen Fuentes knew she would have to escape, not wait for rescue. Her mind raced and she tried to see where they were going. She didn't recognize the area, and her fear heightened. Time wasn't on her side with these two men.

TWO

Lund County Sheriff Dan Halloran's county-issued SUV raced out of the department's parking lot. The description of Macon Baytree's pick-up firmly planted in his mind, he hit his lights and siren, and drove as fast as he dared, headed west through the town square.

Last reported spotting had the souped-up Ford speeding out of Hilldale on the county blacktop that led to Tilson, a small town that once had a river port and rail line, but now squatted forlorn and nearly abandoned, on the banks of the Missouri River.

Old Man Baytree had some acreage just outside of Tilson, and Dan figured he'd be headed for home, looking to take his stand with his son. Their hostage, Carmen Fuentes, insured there'd be no shoot out, at least from law enforcement's side. Baytree appeared to have no sense of fair play, and Dan prepared himself for an "anything goes" stand-off.

"Jeff, how far out are you?" Dan dropped the mic on the seat, needing both hands to negotiate the S curve that took him past Bob Sapp's hay field, the fragrant, neatly cut and raked rows waiting to be baled. *The rain wouldn't help the hay any*, Dan thought as he sped by.

"Right behind you, Sheriff. What's the plan? They might be aiming to hide out at his place west of Tilson."

Safely on a straight stretch of road, Dan triggered his mic. "Let's take this to our agreed secure channel. I've got some ideas but don't want to share them with the world." With that, he moved to the secure channel and hoped if Baytree had a radio on, he wouldn't find them before Dan instructed his deputy on entering the Baytree place from the rear. He hoped to sneak up on the old farmhouse without being seen.

The radio came to life again. "Randy here. Where do you want me? I'm about six miles down route M. We going into Tilson?"

"Take the Frog Hollow road to the back of the farm. We'll spread out. There's an old hay road just before the gates that lead to the horse barn where we found the horses he tried to hide from the Rocheport farm."

Dan took the turn onto the gravel road. Slowing to avoid skidding out of control on the loose rock, he saw a dark pile of what looked like dirty wet rags in the ditch ahead. An old paint mare stood still, head hanging low.

Pumping his brakes, he slid to a stop, his heart thumping, bile burning his throat. Dark teakwood skin stretched tight across his face, glistening with fear. The pile of sodden rags was the body of his dear Kickapoo friend, his wife's grandfather, Billy Sumday.

THREE

Carmen Fuentes huddled in the corner of the bedroom, her mind racing. She surveyed her surroundings. There had to be a way out. Locked in a room right out of the '20's, the musty smell of mold and mouse infestation nearly gagged her.

Flowered wallpaper hung in faded, stained strips. The ceiling, covered in brown water-stains and broken plaster exposed the ancient lattice-work of lathe, and the hand-braided area rug lost its color beneath years of accumulated dust.

Cobwebs stirred and sighed, and the tattered lace curtains did little to hide the daunting sight of old wooden shutters locked securely across the tall narrow windows, bringing dusk into what should have been a bright, rain-washed morning.

A sagging bed with its antique iron headboard and faded dusty quilt that looked as though it had nested several generations of mice, a wobbly rocking chair, and an old highboy dresser filled the small room. On the wall near the door hung six wooden pegs, and a cracked mirror that reflected her image, warped and broken. Pulling her eyes from the distorted refection, she scanned the room, searching for a weapon.

She could break apart the rocker, use parts of it for trying to knock out whoever entered first. If the two men came in together, Carmen knew she couldn't take them both out before they overpowered her.

Before she could decide what to do, a key scraped in the old iron lock, and the heavy porcelain knob jiggled. Her heart skipped a beat.

Macon Baytree pushed through the door and quickly closed it behind him, never taking his eyes off her. Long, stringy, dirty blond hair, in need of washing, hung limply about his narrow face. Bloodshot blue eyes ran up and down her body and he licked his thin lips. Reading his intent sent fear coursing through her. Time was up. She'd have to fight.

Pulling off her stiletto heels, she stood on the wood floor, feet slightly apart, heels in hand. Grinning, Macon crept toward her, his eyes making promises she hoped he wouldn't be able to keep.

Within striking distance, Carmen hurled a heel as hard as she could, aiming at Macon's head. He batted it aside, an ugly sneer curling his lips.

"Sure do like a woman who plays hard to get," he growled. "Gonna make you pay for messing up Pa's appeal. Gonna make you wish you was back in your own country. Them there fancy clothes and lawyer papers don't make you one of us. You gonna wish you never come 'cross the Rio Grande."

Carmen froze. His hatred and ill intent hit her like icy water. Stilling her breathing, she tightened her grip on the remaining heel. Macon's fist lashed out aiming for the center of her face. She swung the long narrow heel driving it with all her strength into his forearm. His fist, thrown off course a bit, missed breaking her nose and connected hard with the side of her head, the full force of the blow landing on her temple.

Struggling to stay on her feet, to pull the embedded heel from the screaming man's arm, the blow to her head overwhelmed her. Nausea threatened. Dizzy, she felt numbness spreading rapidly through her head. Sagging to the floor, the last thing she saw before darkness took her, was James Baytree raging into the room, gun in hand. Carmen slid into the black abyss.

FOUR

Dan radioed for LifeFlite. He found a weak pulse in Billy's neck, but his body lay still, his flesh cold and pale. It looked as though the mare Billy loved so much had turned on him, kicked him nearly to death.

Fury burned through him. Turning to the animal who shied away from him, he grabbed for the dangling reins. He'd have to get Betsy DeGroat, a vet, and head of the bi-county animal rescue, to come get the horse.

As the mare pulled away from him, Dan saw blood seeping from what appeared to be a bullet wound in her side, and another in her shoulder. Foreboding filled him.

Turning back to Billy, he looked closer at the man's visible wounds. Elongated bruises and welts marked his face and neck. A deep gash on the side of his head, long and straight, black with caked blood, told Dan it wasn't the mare who'd kicked his old friend. Someone had beaten him with what looked like a crow bar. He heard the chopper skimming toward them and stepping into the road, he waved them in.

Back in his cruiser, Dan radioed his deputies to check out the Baytree property, see if the father and son were holed up in the old farmhouse or one of the many outbuildings. He informed them he'd found Billy Sumday critically wounded, and would be heading to the University Intensive Care tower.

"Keep me in the loop, Randy. For now, you and Jeff take the lead on this. Call Boone and Cole County for back-up, if you need it. We can't let the Baytree men get too far ahead of us.

"Right now, I've got to call Molly, tell her about her grandfather before she gets the news from someone else." Picking up his cell phone, he hit the button that fast-dialed his wife, dreading the moment she answered.

FIVE

Billy Sumday struggled to swim from the nightmare that held him in its grip. Each breath took him to a place of pain he'd never known before, and he seemed trapped beneath thick dark water that refused to let him rise to the surface.

Pushing himself toward the light pulsing far above him, he cried out as fire coursed through his broken body. No good. He couldn't make it. Where was his mare, Nonhelema? Had Baytree killed her?

A moment of peace swept over him. The mare had fought to save him. Years before, having survived horrific abuse at the hands of the same madman, she'd blossomed and come to trust him. Sacrificing her own safety, Nonhelema had kicked and bit at the young man who'd tried to kill him, and she'd driven him off.

A beeping sound confused him. How could he hear that under water? Where was it coming from? A burning pain ripped through him from his feet to his shoulders and searing into his head. He bit his lip trying not to cry out, but he couldn't hold it back. Agonizing pain. Fire. His legs and arms were on fire. Trying, he couldn't lift his head. Sinking. He felt himself sinking while the pain torpedoed through his brain.

As Billy gave himself up to the agony, a gentle touch caressed his face. He heard a soft whisper calling him from his dark place of torture. Relief swept through him.

Not alone. I'm not alone.

*** * * * ***

Tears burned hot down Molly Halloran's cheeks. Gently, she stroked her grandfather's bruised and broken face. His bandaged head showed the swelling, while his right arm and both legs were encased in soft casts, awaiting surgery when the doctors deemed him able to survive the rigors of the operating room.

Her grandfather's eyelids struggled to open. He cried out in pain, and she watched as his body twitched, trying to free itself from the gauze and tape prison holding it, trying to fend off a phantom attacker.

Weeping, Molly whispered loving words, stroked his bruised cheek, called his name, assuring him she would stay with him. He would not be alone.

A Physician's Assistant at Dr. Abraham Ridley's clinic in Hilldale, Molly knew her grandfather's condition was critical. She knew the chance of him recovering, of being the man he was before the attack were impossible. At ninety-years old, she also knew her grandfather wouldn't want to be kept alive in a nursing home, if an invalid life lay before him. But, Molly couldn't say farewell. Not yet. Not now.

SIX

Carmen opened her eyes. Her jaw ached, and when she tried to move her head, nausea washed over her. Carefully moving her hands, she checked her face, her head. Swelling engulfed the entire left side of her face. It hurt to lift her head from the floor where she'd fallen, and when she tried to sit up, her ribs screamed in protest.

Eyes still clamped shut, she prayed. What had James Baytree done to her? She couldn't remember anything after he'd stormed through the door. Was she shot?

Her hands explored her ribs and came back dry. No blood. Eyes still closed, she listened. Nothing but the silence of an empty house, and birds chirping and singing outside the shuttered windows.

Slowly, she opened her eyes. The room spun, but Carmen forced herself to take a few deep breaths, gasping when the expansion of her lungs caused extreme pain. *Broken ribs, then.*

Eyes open, but staring at the ceiling, she examined the rest of her body, trying to keep panic and pain from overwhelming her. Then it hit her. Her exploring hands met naked flesh. Rolling to her side, she vomited. Darkness claimed her and she welcomed the void as it sucked her in.

When she woke up, the room still held the dregs of late afternoon. The light that struggled to seep past the cracks in the closed shutters told her the day was nearly gone, and her rescuers had not arrived. Hope faded. *Don't give up,* she ordered herself. Thirsty, she tried working up saliva, but the vile taste in her mouth brought back the nausea.

Lifting her head, she looked down the length of her body. Ugly purple bruises darkened her torso, thighs, ribs, even her chest. Rage and fear warred for dominance. Tears threatened, but Carmen Fuentes swallowed them, forced them away. She would not give them the satisfaction of her tears. No matter what. Never.

She forced herself to ignore her pain, and sit up. After the room settled down and the nausea lessened, she got on her hands and knees and pushed herself into standing. The results were immediate. Her body tilted and swayed of its own accord, and bile shot from her mouth. Crumbling to the rug beneath her, she managed to drag the filthy quilt from the bed as she tumbled down, pulling it around her. Once again, the spinning darkness took her.

SEVEN

Hilldale Farewell

Justin Taylor strode down the long tiled hallway that bisected the dank basement of the Lund County Courthouse. The heels of his hand-tooled leather cowboy boots rapped out a staccato beat on the worn, yellowed tiles, echoing his unwavering resolve.

His six-feet, four-inch height, along with his slightly more than two-hundred-pound weight, sat well on a big-boned frame, muscles well defined through the light cotton, western-styled denim jacket open over a white shirt. A bolo tie snugged against his corded neck.

Not a body-builder, as most folks assumed, his body stayed honed by working his father's Brahma/Herford-crossed cattle on the Double T ranch. On his off-duty days, he put in long hard hours riding, roping, working miles of fences, whatever and wherever he was needed.

He tugged at the silver Brahma head that kept the bolo hitched up, loosening it just enough to accommodate his complaining Adam's apple.

Texas-born and ranch-hand raised, Justin found himself a bit claustrophobic in the small town of Hilldale, Missouri. Used to the wide-open range, wind and water stunted sparse trees, and endless sky of west Texas, the town square with its huge oaks and two-story buildings rectangling the one-way street, boxing in the murmuring fountain, made him lonesome for home.

Near the end of the hallway, he stopped in front of the door marked **Custodian**. Tapping lightly, he pushed through the entrance and grinned at the man behind the battered desk.

Nearing sixty, the man's Hispanic features, his still-black hair, and wiry body gave him the appearance of a much younger man. Standing, he opened his arms in welcome. The Marshall never hesitated.

"Señor Fuentes!" Justin stepped around the desk and embraced the much smaller man, the two appearing long familiar with the gesture.

"Ah, Justin, you have come, as promised. It is bad, this kidnapping of my daughter. The sheriff and deputies are doing all they can, I know this, but it is not enough. Soon, three nights will have gone by and my beloved Carmen is still in the hands of those animals."

Justin released his friend and Manuel motioned him to the chair across from his desk. When the younger man settled, he pulled his Stetson from his head and dropped it next to his chair. Stretching out his long legs, he nodded his readiness to listen.

"Start at the beginning and tell me everything you know about what happened. Don't leave out anything, even if you don't think it's connected or helpful—tell me everything, my friend."

Hilldale Farewell

Manuel nodded, and after pouring them each a tall glass of iced tea from the fridge behind his desk, he related as much as he knew about the kidnapping, his hands shaking, his black eyes snapping with anger and fear. Gripping the arms of his chair, he held Justin's gaze with his, his pain naked and raw.

"You must find her before they do more harm to her, you understand?" He hesitated, then finished with, "They are animals, Justin. They will not stop with taking her honor, but when she is no longer useful to them, they will take her life, as well. But you, you have not stopped loving my beautiful willful daughter. I know this. You will not allow what these filthy pigs do to her, to stop that love."

Desperation filled his eyes. His voice dropped as he repeated, "You will still love her, yes?" He tried sipping his tea, but his trembling hand betrayed him and the icy liquid rolled down his chin onto his uniform shirt.

Slumping in his chair, Justin pushed his large calloused hands through his thick brown waves and nodded.

"When she left last year, I thought I could move on, find another. But," his eyes caught the old man's and held them, "I can't. I've loved that stubborn, sassy woman since she was five and pushed me into a load of cattle manure when I tried to kiss her!" A smile twitched at the corner of his mouth.

"When I do find her, I'm going to try to convince her to come home to Texas.

"Those were great days when you and your family lived at the ranch, and you helped doctor the cattle. We were like one family." He rubbed his eyes and studied the older man across from him.

"I'll find her, and yes, I will still love her as much or more than I do now, but that's not the problem, is it? Does she love me? She's the one who left. The one who wanted to be independent, who wanted to make it on her own."

He thought of the dark-haired beauty, with her snapping black eyes, high cheek bones, lips he longed to claim. Shaking off the memories, he turned his attention back to the man behind the desk.

Sighing, Manuel nodded agreement. "Carmen is full of fire. She lives her life like there will be no tomorrow for her." His voice broke at the implication of his words.

"She loves you, *mi amigo*, she just needs to be reminded, yes?" A small smile etched across his weary face. "And you, my friend, are you not as stubborn as my Carmen?"

Justin laughed. Standing, he clapped his Stetson on his head, cocking it over his right eye.

"I'll mosey on over to the sheriff's department and see what they have to offer. They may not appreciate an outsider nosing into their case, but regardless, I'm here to find Carmen. I won't leave until I do. That's a promise. My father has plenty of help, and the U. S. Marshall's office has given me leave of absence, and if I need them, offered their resources.

"My boss already called ahead to warn them I was on my way and had a personal interest in the case. Reckon that won't sit real well with the locals, but I'll try to stay out of their way, if they stay out of mine." Determination set his jaw, and darkened his green eyes to a deep emerald.

EIGHT

Muley Burger sat next to the hospital bed and watched his old friend struggle to breathe. He studied the battered face and body lying fitfully, tubes and wires giving him the appearance of a mangled marionette. He rubbed his whiskers and wished he knew how to pray better.

Billy Sumday cried out, his drug-induced dreams turning to nightmares from which there was no escape. Tears leaked from beneath the single exposed, fluttering eyelid. "Mother! Father! Come back," he screamed.

Muley started. Leaning forward, he laid his hand on Billy's forehead, trying to avoid the bandages.

"Shhhh, old friend," he murmured. "I'm here, Billy. Ain't gonna leave you 'cept to use the outhouse. You sleep. I'll watch over you, just like when we was kids. I won't let no one hurt you again."

Billy moaned. He turned his head toward Muley. His un-bandaged eye opened wide, dark and haunted. "Muley?" he rasped. "Help me." Pain and medication drug him back into unconsciousness.

"I'm here," Muley repeated, hoping Billy could hear him. And as he'd done so many times when they were young boys and the nightmares of Billy's past tormented him, he took his old friend's hand, and in a soft, soothing voice, began a story. Only this time, the story was true.

NINE

Molly walked across the shade-darkened hospital room and curled up next to her grandfather, careful of the tubes and wires leading from the various machines and bags down to his body. His left arm lay free of bandages, and she cradled it next to her as she would a baby. Staring across him to the old man sitting next to the bed, she whispered, "Don't stop, Muley. Your talking seems to calm him."

Nodding, Muley studied the young woman's weary face. She rarely left her grandfather's side and looked exhausted.

"Get some sleep 'fore you ain't no good to no one. I ain't going nowhere. I'll tell him another story if'n you'll go to sleep."

A weak smile trembled across her lips, and, just as quickly, faded. Molly nodded. "It's a deal. I am tired, and the coffee didn't do a thing to wake me up, though it's sure got this little guy moving." She patted her swollen abdomen.

Fear shadowed her green eyes. "I'm afraid if I go to sleep he'll leave me, Muley. It's been nearly a week and…" her whisper died away.

Looking at her grandfather, she snuggled closer until her head nearly touched his shoulder. "Tell us a story, Muley," she sighed, and closed her eyes.

Muley cleared his throat and settled back in the chair. "He weren't but six or thereabouts, when Pa found him all sick with fever curled up in our old hollowed-out sycamore tree.

"That there tree was my hiding place most of my childhood, and seeing a strange-looking boy with hair long as a girl's in my tree, made me mad, it did. Didn't know 'til later what that there hair meant to him, and them school folks planning on cutting it off. Would have shamed him something awful."

Muley sat silent, the memory clear as if it just happened. Closing his eyes, he continued, his voice rough with the visions in his head. He'd never told

Billy's story to anyone except his Emily, and as the memories bubbled up, he felt tears burn his eyes.

"In the beginning I weren't too nice. 'Shamed to admit it, but being the only young'un used to having my folks, the farm, and all the hidey holes to myself, I didn't cotton to the idea of sharing it all with another boy.

"But Pa and Ma, they took to Billy right off. When his folks couldn't be found, the state stepped in. They tried to take him off to another boarding school, but my pa put his foot down, and he and Ma made him their legal son."

Molly lifted her head and looked at Muley, surprised.

"I didn't know that. Grampa never told me that. Does my dad know? He's never talked about Grampa's early years. Only that his folks were driven out of Missouri and he was placed in a boarding school with all the other Native American children forcibly taken from their parents."

Muley nodded, scratching his whiskers. "Billy never spoke much about them years. Never found his folks, though we tried for a great long time to trace them. Many from the Kickapoo tribe went on down to Mexico and disappeared. Was a hurtful thing for him, losing his family thataway."

Molly laid her head back on the pillow next to her grandfather. She stroked the least damaged side of his face. "I love you," she said, once again snuggling closer, grunting as her unborn son kicked and turned until he'd settled against his dying great-grandfather.

Closing her eyes, she sighed. "Then what? What happened to Grampa?"

TEN

Dan looked at the U. S. Marshall standing before him. *Determined. This guy's not going to leave easily.* He shuffled the papers on the desk in front of him, tapping them into a neat pile.

The Texan's jaw twitched with pent-up energy, maybe a little anger, but Dan couldn't allow Justin Taylor to run his own investigation and possibly interfere with the rescue of Carmen Fuentes. The man was staring him down, and his words left nothing to Dan's imagination.

"I'm sorry you see it that way, Sheriff, but I'm not asking your permission. I'm offering my services. You're lead, I get that. It's your territory, but I'm not going away. I'll work with you best I can, but I'm going after Carmen with or without your cooperation."

Dan stood behind his desk. "Your boss tells me you're an outstanding U. S. Marshall, due for promotion soon. Also said you have a vested interest in finding Ms. Fuentes.

"I do understand, and sympathize, Marshall Taylor, but you don't know the lay of the land, and there's a good possibility you could do Ms. Fuentes more harm than good. We know the men who've kidnapped her, we have a pretty good idea where they're hiding out…"

Justin cut him short. "It's been close to a week now, and if I understand the information given me, they're not where you thought they would be, and you really have no idea where they've gone." He raised a dark eyebrow. No question, no backing down.

"Tracking is my specialty. Set me up as a temporary deputy, or whatever you need to do. Point me to a desk in a corner somewhere and let me do what I'm good at." He slapped his Stetson against his leg. "I'm not going away. Not without Carmen."

Studying Justin's expression, Dan knew it was true. Love. This Texas U. S. Marshall obviously loved Ms. Fuentes, and the sheriff could understand his determination. The man wasn't going away, and it made sense to give him something to keep him busy while they looked for the Baytree men, and rescued the public defender.

"Okay, you've convinced me, Marshall Taylor."

"Justin, please. Thanks, Sheriff. It'll be better all the way around if we work together."

Dan grinned. "Right. I think I've got that figured out, Justin. Call me Dan. You can pick one of the three empty desks at the back of the deputy's office. Find Randy Carter and let him know what you need. I'll deputize you and let the staff know what's going on." He reached across the desk and offered his hand.

"Thanks, Dan," Justin said, shaking the sheriff's hand. "You won't regret it."

"Hope not. I suspect you'll do fine. Just try not to run off on your own, and keep us in the loop with what you find. We'll do the same for you."

Nodding, Justin settled his Stetson on his head. "Know a good place to stay close by?"

"Only place in town is Lolly's Bed and Breakfast. Not sure if she's got an opening or not. If you don't mind being out in the boonies a bit, I have a place east of Hilldale you can use while you're here. I live in town with my wife, but still have my acreage with a few head of cattle. You're welcome to stay there."

"Sounds great," Justin smiled. "Gets a mite claustrophobic here in town. I'd appreciate being out in the country."

Dan grinned back at the Texan. "I'll take you out there and get you settled in. There's canned goods, but anything fresh you want you'll need to pick up at the grocery store a few blocks west of here." Turning serious, he stood and moved around the desk stopping in front of the taller man. "We'll find her, Justin."

"Yes, we will," the U. S. Marshall agreed, his jaw clenching. He followed Dan from the office. A desk, a place to stay. Justin Taylor silently called out to the love of his life, praying she would hear and be strong. He was coming to rescue her—soon.

ELEVEN

"Muley?"

Muley Burger sat up. The recliner squawked in protest as he lowered the leg rest and pulled the blanket from around him. Stiffness had settled into his hips and knees. Struggling to stand, he heard the hoarse whisper again.

"Muley?" An agonized cough followed and Muley leaned over the bed where Billy lay staring up at him, his one good eye open, black obsidian glowing in the dim light of the room.

"Molly?"

Muley shook his head. "Ain't here. I sent her home for a shower and sleep. Don't need a shower myself, and this here chair sleeps fine. Told that young'un to get on back to her husband. Didn't want to go, but promised her I'd stay right here and call her the minute you woke up."

He winked. "Been using your outhouse 'stead of the one down the hallway. Ain't gonna tell on me, are you?"

The old man pulled a cell phone from his pocket and waved it before Billy's face. "Lookie here," he grinned, "got me one of them pocket phones like the kids use. Gordie brought it home and he's been helping me figure the dadburn thing out. Sure is handy once I got the hang of it. Right addicting, it is."

Flipping open the top, he began to punch in numbers. Billy groaned. "Stop!" he rasped, his words halting and breathless. "Let her rest, spend time with Daniel. Got to talk to you."

Again, a violent cough erupted. Blood trickled from Billy's mouth and Muley grabbed a tissue from the bed stand and gently wiped it away.

"Quiet, you ornery old man. Got yourself beat up good, you did. Reckon that old mare saved your life. Took a couple of bullets for you. Vet took them out and Little Wanda and Gordie's doctoring her.

"Him and Juanita's gotta work mighty hard to get Little Wanda to come in the house. Spends every waking moment with that bag of bones horse of yours. Gordie found her sleeping next to her, Nonhelema laying ever so still, careful not to hurt that there wee child. Beats anything I ever saw."

Billy tried to smile but it quickly turned into a grimace. Shifting as much as his imprisoned body would allow, he reached out his good hand and Muley held it.

"Baytree boy. Tell Daniel." Gasping, he squeezed his eye closed breathing hard against the pain that tore through him. When it passed, he looked at his old friend, his adopted brother.

"Need you to tell Oscar why I left him with Emma up at Red Lake, after his mother died. Tell him the truth. Got a will at the cabin in the strong box. Most goes to my son and granddaughter, a few things for Little Wanda. Tell Oscar…" Billy gasped hard trying to talk to Muley, but pain and exhaustion pulled him back into their embrace.

Shaking his head at the unconscious man, Muley sank back into the recliner. "Ain't gonna do that, old friend. Never told no one and ain't gonna start now."

The pump that dispensed morphine into Billy's bloodstream whirred, sending the drops of pain medicine through the tubing into his blood vein.

Muley wept.

TWELVE

Screams echoed from somewhere outside her room. Carmen sat up, her hair prickling at the tortured cry.

She tugged the quilt around her shoulders, straining to listen.

"Pa! Help me, my arm's on fire. I'm freezing—burning—help me, Pa. I hurt so bad." More agonized cries and words she couldn't make out. Then she heard James Baytree's voice trying to calm his son.

She remembered driving the spiked heel of her shoe into Macon Baytree's arm as he delivered a powerful blow to the side of her head. The rest of her memories were jumbled into a tangled mess she didn't want to sort out. Her ribs protested when she shifted to sit at the side of the bed.

Must be night, she thought realizing the room lay in dark shadows. Struggling against the pain in her body and in her mind, Carmen pushed herself to a wobbly standing position. Gasping, she wiped the beads of sweat from her forehead. Her teeth clenched against the agony that seared her chest.

"I will survive," she whispered into the darkness. "They will not defeat me." She'd had little food and water since her capture. She wasn't hungry, but she longed for a cool drink to rinse her mouth and ease the dryness in her throat.

She thought of her father. He must be frantic with worry. Her mind turned to Justin Taylor, the man she hoped to marry one day. Would her father call him? Would he come? She'd left him to pursue her dream of being a lawyer, standing on her own. Closing her eyes, she pictured his face, heard his voice.

Carmine shook herself from her reverie. Her face burned where the droplets of sweat caught, and when she tried to dab the moisture away, she realized her nose was broken and her right eye painfully swollen. *A new beating.*

Tears threatened and she refused to think of what Baytree had done to her. Even in the darkness, Carmen closed her eyes against the memory—the smell and feel of him. She would not cry.

"I will survive," her voice trembled with emotion. This time, she didn't whisper.

THIRTEEN

Little Wanda lay curled against Nonhelema's chest. The paint mare shifted and nuzzled her, causing her to giggle. Rolling to her knees, she buried her small hands in the horse's mane, and pressed her forehead against Nonhelema's.

Softly, Little Wanda began to sing a song from somewhere in her dreams she'd heard Grampa Billy sing. A song of healing, of grass thick and tall; streams of water, cold and pure; of wild herds racing the winds across the endless prairies.

The paint mare listened and closed her eyes to sleep. The pain in her side and shoulder lessened, and her dreams were no longer nightmares. The tiny human stroked her face and neck, then rose to her feet and moved to her side.

Nonhelema felt the small hands press gently but firmly against her wounds, and at first this startled her awake, but then the warmth and tingling penetrated her hide and once again, in peace, she slept.

Little Wanda ran to the house where her father and mother sat quietly talking at the kitchen table, their breakfast dishes ready to be cleared, the child's plate still full.

When she hopped up on her chair her mother scolded, "Wash those hands, young lady. You've been in the barn all night. Wash up at the sink and you can have a bath and get clean clothes when you've finished eating your breakfast. Warm your bacon and eggs?" Juanita Bently raised an eyebrow and smiled.

Her father moved a stool to the sink and Little Wanda climbed up to wash her hands. A quick swipe at the towel, and back to the table she went, making short work of her breakfast, informing her parents of her night and morning with the wounded mare.

"I sang her the healing song Grampa Billy sings, and Nonhelema went to sleep just like I do when he sings to me." She looked troubled for a moment. "He won't be singing to me anymore."

Shaking her head as if to rid herself of the sad thoughts, she shoveled the last of her scrambled eggs into her mouth, and drank from her glass of milk.

"She's getting better, Papa, because I know the healing song. I listened and I learned it just the way Grampa Billy does it."

Gordie Bently looked at his wife and smiled. "Reckon she got her singing talent from me seeing as you have trouble finding the notes you want." He laughed as Juanita lightly smacked his arm. Little Wanda watched her parents and grinned.

"Do I have to change, Ma? I'm going to do my chores and go right back to the barn. Means I'll just get dirty all over again." She studied her mother and waited.

Juanita laughed and reached for her daughter. She hugged her close and inhaled the clean smell of the barn, picked a piece of straw from her red curls, and hugged her again. Little Wanda snuggled close.

"Yes you do have to take a bath and change your clothes before you go back out to the barn. You don't want Nonhelema to faint from smelling you, do you?"

Little Wanda threw back her head and laughed. "Oh, Ma, horses don't faint. At least, not this one. She's named after the Shawnee warrior woman, and she saved Grampa Billy's life—for a little while."

Her mother lifted her from her lap. "No matter, Sugar, you finish cleaning your room, put your folded laundry away, then a bath, and clean clothes. Now march, young lady."

Little Wanda reached up and patted her mother's face, kissed her cheek, and twisted one of her bright red curls around her finger holding it to her own red curls, and grinned. "We match!"

She ran around the table and her father lifted her to his lap. She hugged him and kissed his cheek. Solemnly looking at her parents, she said, "I'm going to be a healer. Grampa Billy won't need the healing song, but a lady is coming, and she's going to need me to sing the healing song to her."

With that, she hopped from her father's lap and headed for the stairs, leaving Gordie and Juanita staring after her.

FOURTEEN

Justin Taylor closed the county plat book. Taking up his notes, he stuffed them in his brief case and left the courthouse records room. He believed he knew where the Baytree men were holding Carmen, and if all went according to his plan, she'd be rescued this very evening.

First stop would be the sheriff's office. He knew Dan might have a little trouble with his proposal, but if he couldn't come up with a better plan, Justin would implement his—with or without the Lund County Sheriff's help.

When he pushed through the glass doors of the Sheriff's department, he nodded at the receptionist and headed straight for Dan's office.

"Morning, Justin." Reaching for his coffee, Dan Halloran pointed toward mugs and the coffee pot behind him. "Help yourself. Vicki baked up some banana bread. I reckon I can share a slice or two with you. What's up?"

"Thanks, I'll pass on the coffee and bread. Got something to show you." He sat across from Dan and opened his brief case, pulled out his notes, and laid them on the desk.

"I believe I know where Carmen is, and I have a plan. Got a map of Calloway County?"

Dan nodded and opened his desk drawer, retrieved a spiral county map book, and placed it in front of Justin. "What are we looking at?"

"Did some checking and found out Macon Baytree's great-grandfather on his mother's side owned some acreage up along a place called Cedar Creek. If I'm not mistaken, that's out past your place?"

The sheriff nodded. "Who we talking about, and what's that got to do with where they're holding Carmen?"

"Fella's name was Jacob Nicholes and he married Anna White. Their granddaughter married Baytree but died giving birth to Macon Baytree. James remarried two more times, both women died from accidents early in the marriage under suspicious circumstances—nothing proven—on the Baytree farm west of town. This place I'm talking about is east out Route Y near a place called Devil's Backbone."

Justin cleared his throat and said, "Nicholes had no other children or grandchildren, and left the place to James to be passed on to Macon. I got a copy of the will."

He sat back and stared at Dan. "She's there. I know it sure as I'm sitting here. I could use some help getting to this place and wondered if you knew the lay of the land there? Any way in that he wouldn't see us coming?"

"Jacob Nicholes?" Dan scratched his chin. "Didn't know about the connection there. Calloway County is not part of my territory, but I'm familiar with the area. Hunt white-tail deer out there. Good work. Reckon you are a good tracker, more ways than one.

"I know the place and there are a few ways in. Last I saw, the home place was boarded up and looked about to fall in. The old wooden bridge across the creek washed out a year or so ago. We'll have to walk in the last bit of the way.

"Let me show you on the map what I'm talking about, then I'll give Hank Thompson a head's up, seeing it's his jurisdiction. He may want to be part of this. Of course, I'll get my deputies to help us.

"We're not going in with guns blazing, Justin. Sure as we do, they'll kill Ms. Fuentes and make a run for it. They know this county like the back of their hand, and I'd rather not lose her or them." He leveled his gaze at the U. S. Marshall.

Justin scowled. "You know I'll do everything in my power to protect her. I set my mind on marrying her when I was nine years old, and that hasn't changed." He sighed. "It's got to be quick and quiet, Dan. And, it's got to be today."

"What if they aren't there?"

"Oh, they're there, all right. Can't explain how I know it, I just do. Sounds crazy, I know, but I'm going in, with or without your help." His chin jutted forward and he clenched his jaw.

Dan pulled the map book toward him, paged through it and found what he wanted. Pushing the book back to Justin he stabbed his index finger down on the page.

"Jacob's place is here. Look to the front of the property and then east and you'll see how the creek crosses the farm. We can get close by boat, and where the creek runs shallow, we can walk the rest of the way. Woods should cover us until we get to the barn. It's all open from there to the house. Could wait 'til dark and hope they're not standing guard."

Justin studied the map and nodded. "Let's go in just before dusk and set up our perimeter before it gets too dark to see what we're doing. Your men know the area?" When Dan nodded, he continued.

"We take the front and back of the house at the same time. I'm hoping to figure out where they're keeping her before we go in. Might get lucky and find out where the two men are. No matter what, I'm going in with whoever you say. No arguments, Dan. I'm going in for her."

FIFTEEN

James Baytree unwrapped the dirty towel from Macon's arm. Burning up with fever, his boy shivered. The putrid odor and green pus told him all he needed to know. The sight of angry red streaks crawling up toward his son's shoulder made him shudder. His boy was dying.

He had to get him to the hospital and soon, but he knew he himself wasn't going back to prison. That meant leaving the boy for the law, if he survived. Baytree knew prison wasn't any picnic, but he couldn't let the boy die without trying to save him. Macon was the only blood family he had left.

"Come on, son, get up. You gotta help me get you to the truck. You need a doctor, boy." Baytree helped the feverish young man to his feet. Unsteady, Macon wrapped his good arm around his father's neck and the two men headed outside to the pickup.

"What about the lawyer woman, Pa? She hurt me real bad."

"Yeah, well she's gonna get hers, boy. Nobody knows where she is. She's locked in, ain't got her clothes, ain't got no food or water. I laid into her with my fists and boots. Reckon she's got herself some broke bones, maybe even a busted gut. She's gonna die, boy, slow and painful. Deserves it, too, after what she done to you. Don't you worry none about her. She ain't going nowhere but straight to the devil."

James keyed the Ford into life and gunned the engine, kicking up a cloud of dust as he sped out the driveway. He forded the shallow creek, and headed down the gravel road toward Columbia.

Baytree's thoughts stewed dark and thick with fury. Hatred seethed, and he felt as if his very bones burned with the heat of it. He was leaving the boy at the emergency entrance of the University Hospital, and then he had some business to take care of with the good folks of Hilldale. They'd remember James Baytree when he got done with them. Yes, they would.

Reaching the highway, he sped through the moonless night, as dark as his thoughts.

SIXTEEN

Molly Halloran read her grandfather's chart, biting her lip trying to keep from crying. He'd been moved from Intensive Care to a private room where family could stay as-long-as they wanted. She knew what that meant—hospice.

Unchecked, tears brimmed over, rolling hot down her cheeks. The baby inside her tumbled and kicked and she laid her hand over her abdomen, calming him.

"Why, God?" she cried silently, her agonized prayer that repeated itself over and over. "He's been Your servant most of his life. How can You let this happen to him?"

Molly fought the anger that threatened to rise against her Heavenly Father. She knew about the suffering of God's followers—she'd read their stories in the bible, in books. But now it was her beloved grandfather, and she felt she couldn't bear the sorrow of his suffering.

Placing the chart back in the carousel, she wiped her tears. In the breakroom, she poured herself a cup of coffee and laced it heavily with cream and sugar. Muley Burger sat with her grandfather while she used the restroom and checked the doctor's notes.

She needed to make a few calls before she went back in the room to give the old farmer a break. Weariness, emotionally and physically, wrapped her in its heaviness.

Muley, who'd been faithful to stay the days and nights Molly had to go home, hadn't been back to the farm in nearly a week. She knew he needed a bath and a change of clothes, whether he wanted to or not. Gordie Bently now owned the place and he, Juanita, and Little Wanda took care of it, but Molly knew Muley needed to take a day away from the hospital.

She called Dan and asked him to drive Muley back to the farm, and to bring her clean clothes for the next few days. She would stay with her grandfather until her father or Muley returned, and then she'd only leave him long enough to spend time with her husband and help him set up the nursery. If she was right, their son would arrive before the end of September.

Sadness squeezed her heart. After two miscarriages, she and Dan looked forward to the birth of their son. Molly longed for her grandfather to see him, to hold him, to give him his blessing like he'd done for her when she was born. *Please God*, she prayed silently, *please let him live to meet his great-grandson*.

Back in his room, Molly straightened the sheets and plumped Billy Sumday's pillows. She told Muley that Dan was headed to the hospital to pick him up and take him back to the farm. With a heartfelt hug, she thanked him for staying so long, and for the wonderful stories of her grandfather's early life.

"He'd do the same for me," Muley told her. "'Cept he'd be telling you tall tales and trying to make believe I was a rounder as a young'un." He grinned, and reaching up, hugged her back.

"Love covers a lot, and we had plenty of that growing up with my folks. Reckon we was blessed to have Billy come along, but reckon he was blessed to land at the folks' farm."

An hour later, Dan entered the room and Muley pushed himself from his chair, stepped to the bed, and patted Billy's hand. "Be back quicker 'en you can skin a rattlesnake." He waited while the sheriff hugged his wife and helped her put her clothes in the closet.

Dan leaned over the bed softly speaking to Billy, then prayed over him before he turned back to his wife. Hugging Molly again, he and Muley headed out to his truck.

Voice rough with sorrow, Muley looked at his young friend as he drove from the parking lot.

"Looking like Billy's going to have a tough row to hoe." He stared out the windshield and watched Columbia's lights fade as they headed out of town toward Hilldale. "Folks is praying, but maybe God's answer ain't what we want. I'm older'n him and should go on ahead." A tear rolled down his cheek and lost its way in the old man's days-old whiskers.

Dan watched the traffic as he turned off Stadium Road and headed south on highway 63. Molly kept him up on the lack of progress in her grandfather's recovery, and she'd wept in his arms as the two prayed for Billy's healing, at least enough to come live with them, let them care for him for whatever days the Lord granted him. She longed for her grandfather to hold their son, and Dan longed for it, too.

Kickapoo Billy Sumday had always been in his life, always been there as he grew up, him and Muley being the father to him his own couldn't be. The love they showed him countered the abuse and angry words his father showered over him and his mother, nearly drowning them in his bitterness and anger fueled by the alcohol that eventually destroyed his brain and liver.

Dan shook off the dark thoughts. He'd forgiven his father, let the past go, and when it tiptoed back, trying to sneak its way into his heart and mind, he cast it away.

He set his mind on prayers for Billy, and for his wife who mourned for the life seeping from her beloved grandfather. He prayed for comfort. He prayed for peace. And he prayed for his unborn son to arrive in time to meet his namesake.

SEVENTEEN

Dan informed his men that the Calloway County Sheriff had turned the rescue/arrest over to them. He and two of his deputies, Randy Carter and Jeff Springer, clustered around the deputies' desks and listened as Justin Taylor explained how he thought they could rescue the public defender, and hopefully capture the Baytree men. Showing them the map, they all agreed taking the farm from the front and back was best, and then Justin stopped and looked at each man.

"I'm going in first, going to try to see if I can figure out where in the house she's being held. Carmen is my main priority. Her safety is our number one concern over capturing the Baytree men."

His lips formed a grim line and his jaw muscles bulged. "They will be captured, one way or another, that I promise you." The men sat silent before the U. S. Marshall's deadly calm.

Dan nodded. "I'm with you on this, Justin, but you have a team behind you, don't forget that and play the lone cowboy. Straight talk, now. Don't try to do it all on your own. We're good at our job, we know the area, and we all want Ms. Fuentes out safe and sound." The gentleness in his voice took some of the sting from his words. Still, the Marshall winced.

"I understand, Sheriff, but let me reconnoiter the house before we storm the place. We've a better chance at saving her if we know where she's at. And, I'm going in first."

Again, Dan nodded. "You do that, and we'll keep watch until you give the word."

Justin studied the map once more and then stood and clapped his Stetson on his head. "Time to go. Carmen's waiting on us."

EIGHTEEN

Sheriff Dan and his deputies anchored the boat and climbed to shore, Justin right behind them. They checked their weapons and quietly rehearsed their roles in the hopeful rescue and takedown at the farmhouse. Dan pointed out Justin's route and the men separated, moving stealthily through the timber and brush that surrounded the seemingly abandoned property.

Dusk dropped gently, and the late August evening lay soft and warm with just a whisper of breeze to keep the swarms of gnats from overwhelming them. Each man found his place and settled in to wait for Justin's signal.

The old clapboard house, and the weathered-oak barn lay in a rough, weed-infested circle of what was once a yard. A few cottonwood trees provided cover for them, and they kept low to the ground using the gooseberry brambles and sumac bushes to stay out of sight. The U. S. Marshall stopped behind a straggly old lilac bush, its branches bent and twisted. He studied the rear of the dark farm house waiting for any sign of movement, any sign they'd been seen.

"No light visible from here. Any of you see anything? Truck is gone." His whisper entered the other men's earpieces and each responded with the same negative sighting.

"Looks like this isn't the place," Dan whispered back.

"It's the place." Justin's hushed voice replied. "Baytree or the son may have gone for supplies. I'm betting they're both gone. No lights, no vehicle, but I've got fresh tracks back here and they look like they're from a truck. Carmen's in there, Dan. I know it. I'm going in for a closer look. Let me know if you see anything from your places."

"You got it, Justin. Watch yourself. We'll be there the second we get your signal, so don't play lone wolf, okay?"

"Holding to the plan, Sheriff. I'm going in."

The back of the house lay silent and shadows played games with his vision. Justin crouched at the back of the building nearest what he believed to be a bedroom. Most old farmhouses were built with the same, or similar, layout. Heavy wooden shutters covered the windows, and even where the spaces between the boards were, darkness prevailed.

Hilldale Farewell

Moving closer, he mounted what he guessed was the milk porch steps, and he knew they usually led to the kitchen. A soft creak from the old boards brought him to a dead stop. Waiting, sweat trickling down his back, he listened for any sounds that meant he'd been heard. Nothing.

Letting go of the breath he'd been holding, he noted the screen door hanging by the top hinge. With minimal movement, there was just enough space for him to sidle between it and the closed storm door. Justin tested the old wooden door's latch and found it locked. Disappointment rolled through him. Then he heard it.

"Dan, she's in here, back room to the right of the milk porch. Sounds like she's in a lot of pain, but she's talking out loud. Don't think there's anyone else in there. I'm going through the back door and need you right behind me just in case."

"Got it," Dan replied. "Randy, stay in front in case one of them is in there and decides to make a run for it. Jeff, take the left side of the house. I'm going in behind Justin."

The men heard a crash as Justin broke the door's lock, saw the glow of the Marshall's flashlight, and heard his warning call to whoever might be hiding in the farmhouse. The hair prickled on the men's necks when they heard Carmen Fuentes' terrible cry for help pierce the night.

Rushing inside, the sheriff and his deputies followed the light into the back bedroom. They found Justin hunched over on his knees attending to the quilt-wrapped bundle on the floor. The terrible stench, and the look he gave them over his shoulder kept them back, and had Dan on his cell phone calling for an ambulance.

Before he hit **end** on his cell, Gina, his night receptionist informed him that Macon Baytree had been admitted to the University hospital in critical condition, and that the father fled after dropping off his son. Dan acknowledged the information, ordered security for Billy Sumday, and looked at Justin.

"You copy that?"

Nodding, the Marshall replied, "We need a chopper here. Ambulance will be too rough on these roads and take too long. Better call your LifeFlite folks."

The sheriff moved to where he could see Carmen. Talking into his cell, he ordered the helicopter and backed away, taking his deputies with him. From what he could see, it would be a miracle if Carmen Fuentes survived.

NINETEEN

Hope failed her. As Molly read her grandfather's updated medical notes, she realized the truth. It would take a miracle for him to live much longer, and she also realized, his suffering grew each day he lived.

His kidneys had stopped functioning, his broken bones couldn't be set properly, his right lung punctured—on and on went the report. Weeping, she replaced his file and nodded to the RN on duty.

"Thanks, Ruth," she whispered, "it's not good news, is it?"

Ruth Hanson walked over to Molly and wrapped her arms around her. As she held the weeping woman, she prayed for wisdom, for the right words of comfort.

"How you doing? Your patients sure miss you since you took your leave of absence from the clinic. Looks like it won't be long before junior is born." She kept her arms around her friend, speaking words of encouragement.

"Listen, if God allows him to live, He'll give him the strength to go through this suffering. I know your grandfather, and he loves his Lord. Leave the battle to them, and you hold fast to that love you have. I know he's grateful for you being here, and I know that your love is a salve for his weary heart. Stand fast, Molly. You all are in our prayers."

Molly nodded and reached for a tissue on the desk. Wiping her eyes and nose, she took a deep breath. "Thank you, again, Ruth. You are a blessing. I'm glad you're working this unit. God is in the details and I must keep reminding myself of that. It's so hard watching him struggle, and I feel selfish that I don't want him to go.

"Dad's with him, and in an hour, he has a class to teach at the U. I'd better get back to Grandpa's room." Another quick hug, and she headed down the long hallway.

When she entered Billy Sumday's room, her heart skipped a beat. Her father was gone, and a hospital security guard sat in the chair next to her grandfather's bed, reading a magazine. He stood to greet her.

"Mrs. Halloran? I'm Jake Sandler. I work for the hospital." Noting her late term pregnancy, he took her arm. "Here, sit down, please." He led her to a nearby easy chair.

"What's going on? Where's my father, Oscar Sumday? What are you doing here?"

Jake sat across from her and lowered his voice. "He left when I got here about an hour ago. Macon Baytree was admitted through the emergency room. It appears his father dropped him off and left. He's in pretty bad shape—the boy, not the father. Don't have any details, but your husband was notified and he requested security for your grandfather, just in case."

Fear ran hot through her and Molly's hands began to shake. "He's here? Where's the father? Did they catch him?"

"Gone," responded the guard shaking his head. "No sign of him. He just dropped off the kid. Didn't wait to get help, just dumped him outside ER and drove off. The boy might not make it, is what I hear."

Nodding, Molly leaned back in her chair, closed her eyes, and took in a deep breath. Dan would make sure her grandfather stayed safe, she knew this, but the idea of the man who inflicted all this damage on him being in the same hospital frightened and angered her.

Molly Halloran was ashamed to admit she wanted Macon Baytree dead, and she believed she could strike the first blow.

TWENTY

Justin held Carmen's hand as the men loaded her into the helicopter. Climbing aboard, he brooked no protests but settled next to the secured stretcher, out of the way of the medical personnel, but close enough that Carmen could see him should she open her eyes.

"Buckle up," ordered the pilot, and along with the other medics made ready for the flight to the University Hospital in Columbia. One started inserting drip-lines and IV's to try and stabilize the patient. Every touch brought a moan of agony from her, but no tears.

The Physician's Assistant doing triage, spoke softly in the microphone connecting him to the hospital. "Multiple bone breaks, apparent ribs included. Left lung sounds like fluid invasion. Multiple lacerations and deep bruising to face and body, broken nose. Dehydration, probable lack of food. Difficult to start IV but got one in and hoping the vein holds. ETA in seven minutes."

Horror washed over Justin, and rage came hot on its heels. Looking at Carmen, her eyes closed, her breathing too rapid and shallow, he wanted to weep. And he wanted to kill the Baytree men.

Something in him stilled to a deadly quiet. United States Marshall Justin Taylor knew he would not leave the two men alive.

TWENTY-ONE

Molly woke up to the ragged whisper of her grandfather's voice calling her name. His good arm lifted and he struggled to hold his hand out to her. She removed his oxygen mask.

"Granddaughter! Molly, take my hand and place it on the child. It's time."

She took his hand and sat up enough to position it over her unborn son's body lying still in her womb. His hand, warm with fever, settled over

William Daniel Halloran and the boy shifted, pushing out against the gentle pressure.

Billy Sumday began the blessing chant, then gave the child his personal blessing, in the name of his Savior, Jesus. As he prayed, his voice strengthened. The baby kicked out, pushing against his great-grandfather's hand, as though agreeing with all spoken over him.

Molly wept, her hand covering her grandfather's, knowing this was his rally before he sank into death, his spirit freed from the worn garment of this life.

When Kickapoo Billy Sumday finished, he slipped his hand from beneath Molly's and briefly laid it atop hers.

"I love you, Granddaughter. Rough water's ahead, but trust that rescue is sure. Your son will touch many hearts and bring peace to many troubled minds. Do not waver from your faith, child, for God is faithful to bring you through the fire. Forgive, that you be forgiven. You and your love have been a blessing to me."

His voice faded, then feebly, he repeated, "I love you, Granddaughter. Tell your father, Muley and the kids, and Daniel, I love them and I am grateful for them being in my life. Give Little Wanda my medicine bag. She'll know…"

His hand clutched at hers, went limp, and slid down to the bed. Kickapoo Billy Sumday slipped away to cross the Jordan into the Promised Land.

Most of the town of Hilldale turned out to pay their respects to Billy. His memorial was held in the high school gymnasium. So many people came forward to share how Billy Sumday had helped them in one way or another, Pastor Hughes never gave his eulogy. Gordie sang *Rock of Ages* and *Be Still My Soul]*, two of Billy's favorite hymns, bringing the funeral to a close.

Carter and Tina Neely opened the café and offered lunch to all who wanted to gather in Billy's memory. Oscar and Lydia Sumday, along with Molly and Dan, sat with the people who loved him, and the stories they told brought tears and laughter, easing the pain of their loss.

TWENTY-TWO

James Baytree stood at the edge of the overgrown woods and watched the raiding of the farmhouse. Cops everywhere. Bright lights making it look like daylight. Disgust and rage warred within him. So much for getting his supplies.

He'd lived rough more than once, and he could do it again. He had resources. He had plans—

big plans for Hilldale. That town would sure enough be sorry they ever messed with the Baytree men.

He thought it a shame he hadn't been able to attend the old Kickapoo's funeral. Send him off with a bang, take a few do-gooders out in the process. Well, he'd make up for the lost opportunity.

Silently, he slipped back into the deeper shadows and walked the mile-and-a-half through the woods back to his truck. He'd have to find other transportation and soon. Plans. Oh, yes, he had plans.

TWENTY-THREE

Manuel Fuentes stood next to his daughter's bed and wept. She'd just returned from recovery after emergency surgery to repair and inflate her punctured lung, and to try to set the worst of the bone breaks in her wrist, ribs, right arm, and face.

More surgeries were in her future, both plastic surgeries and surgeries to pin the worst of the breaks in her arm and wrist. The doctor had informed him, due to extreme damage, they'd had to remove her uterus, right kidney, and spleen.

His shoulders shook with sobs. The ICU nurse squeezed his arm in sympathy before she left him to absorb the damage done to his beloved child.

Manuel looked out the glassed-in enclosure. Justin Taylor slumped in a chair in the hallway, his head leaning against the wall, his long legs stretched out before him, and he appeared to be sleeping.

The young man had called him the minute he'd gotten to the hospital, and had warned him, Carmen had taken a terrible beating and was in surgery. But still, his father's heart and mind had not been prepared for the reality of what lay before him.

He barely recognized his daughter. Wiping his tears and stifling his sobs, he gently touched her hand. Cold. His girl felt so cold and still. Manuel shuddered at the thought of losing his only child.

Her mother had died when Carmen was four and it'd been just the two of them. Living at the Taylor ranch had been like having extended family, and when Carmen told him she was leaving for a job in Missouri, reluctantly, he'd given Justin's father his notice and followed his daughter to Hilldale.

He'd been blessed to get the job as a custodian in the courthouse, and had worked hard. When the head custodian retired last month, he'd been hired to fill the position.

And he was close to his beloved Carmen, able to see her off and on throughout the work days, spending weekends together in the little home they shared. He couldn't see life without his daughter.

Watching the machines breathing for her, rehydrating and feeding her, replacing the blood she'd lost, he felt a shifting in his heart.

Justin had informed him the Baytree boy was in surgery right here in the hospital, abandoned by his father, near death. Manuel felt no sympathy.

He couldn't remember ever hating anyone so much he wanted them dead, but Manuel Fuentes realized, he would do whatever was in his power to do, to end the Baytree men's lives. They must pay for what they'd done to his child, and as her father, it was his duty to avenge her honor, and possibly her life.

TWENTY-FOUR

The white-coat-clad figure nodded to the guard, flashed the ID card hanging from its cord, then entered the ICU room, quickly pulling the curtains closed. Leaning over the bed, the figure studied the unconscious man, the drip-lines, the oxygen hose. Hatred rose like molten lava, burning away fear.

Removing a syringe from the lab coat pocket, the figure pulled back the plunger allowing air to fill the extra-large tube. Expertly inserting the needle into the jugular vein, the plunger sank inward forcing the huge bubble of air into the blood stream. Almost immediately, alarms rang and lights flashed.

The figure stepped back and waited silently in the shadow of the door. When the guard and ICU nurse rushed into the room, their eyes went to the thrashing body of Macon Baytree.

The figure stepped forward as though just coming into the room to help, but as others hurried in, the figure slipped out the door, and turning away from the security cameras, rushed down the hallway and through the stairway door.

Help had arrived within seconds, but a few moments later, the young man no longer needed them.

TWENTY-FIVE

James Baytree checked the backpack. Everything in order. Going still, he listened to the night sounds around him. Nothing out of the ordinary. He settled in the deep shadows, revenge and hatred his dark companions. The good folks of Hilldale would pay for letting his boy die.

He waited for Neely's to close and watched as Carter Neely locked the rear door and headed for his pickup. A minute later, the headlights faded away. He crept through the shadows to the dark side of the building. Smiling, he planted the backpack next to the natural gas line.

Here's my opening shot, folks, and it's just the beginning. This is for my boy, Macon. Now you'll know just who you've been messin' with.

Moving to safety back behind an old oak tree, he pulled a note from his pocket and tacked it to the rough bark. **This is for Macon.** Pulling a detonator from his shirt pocket, he pressed the green button. Within seconds, the rear of Neely's Café was little more than a pile of rubble and roaring flames.

TWENTY-SIX

Carter Neely stood next to Dan as they watched the last of the embers glowing in the smoke-filled early morning light. The two men, lost in their own thoughts of the history and memories that had gone up in flames, were silent before the devastating damage.

"Total loss, Dan," Carter finally spoke, his face slack with weariness. "At least he waited until the place was empty. No lives lost. Probably intended to burn the town down." Bitterness put an edge to his words. Shaking his head, he struggled to keep his emotions in check.

The sheriff studied the ruins of the café smoldering before them. "Reckon you're right. You can rebuild. The town needs Tina and you, and the café. It's where we come to be together, hear the town news. Shoot, I've been coming here most of my life. Don't even think of quitting, Carter."

"I'm tired, ready to retire. Not sure I want to rebuild. Since Juanita left last year to help Gordie on the farm, the place seems to wear Tina and me out. Billy used to help me with the cooking when I needed it, but now he's gone."

The men dropped back into silence, each thinking of the heartbreaking losses the town had taken in less than a month. Carter stared at the debris of his café.

"Baytree is sucking the heart right out of Hilldale, Dan. Killing us, one way or another."

Gritting his teeth, the sheriff said, "We'll get him, believe me. Can't figure out how he knew his boy died unless he got back in the hospital without anyone seeing him. The guard was outside ICU in the hallway. Says only hospital personnel went in or out. Says he checked all ID's. It just went wrong.

"Could be Baytree has someone on the inside keeping him informed about what's going on, but the news folks didn't have the information until the next day."

His hand on Carter's shoulder, he thought of the murder of Billy Sumday, the ferocious attack on Carmen Fuentes, and now the bombing of Neely's Café. To himself as much as to the man beside him, he said, "We'll get him. One way or another, we'll get him."

TWENTY-SEVEN

Carmen stood at the bottom of the porch steps and looked up at the screen door. The sheriff had insisted she stay with this family to hide out from James Baytree. Fear of her attackers, fear of staying in an unfamiliar place, fear of living with strangers, fear of her disfigurements made it difficult for her to breathe.

Justin, carrying her luggage, stepped around her and mounted the steps. A young man appeared behind the screen, dark curly hair tied back into a shoulder-length ponytail. His badly scarred face lit up as he opened the door and grinned at the pair.

"Welcome! Didn't hear you coming but the dogs made such a ruckus figured it was you what arrived." He blushed, and held out his hand to Justin. "Gordie Bently," he said.

"Justin Taylor. Sure appreciate you helping us out here. Where do you want me to take Ms. Fuentes' luggage?"

"Carmen, please." Carmen said, trying not to stare at the scarred young man before her. She lost a little of her own embarrassment as she realized the young man felt shy about his face and deformed fingers.

She'd heard stories about his grandfather beating him, but she'd also heard the stories about how he'd become a beloved citizen of Hilldale, and that he had become a well-known gospel singer. His gentle manner calmed her fear of being in an unfamiliar place.

"Thank you for allowing me to hide out here for awhile. I really appreciate it." She tried to laugh to lighten her words, but it came out hollow and held the sound of her fear.

Gordie nodded, understanding soft in his summer-blue eyes. Pulling open the screen door, he motioned for them to follow him. He led them upstairs to a large bedroom at the end of the hallway.

"Got to share a bathroom with Little Wanda, but she don't make too much a mess—well, not usually." He laughed. "She's seven, but reckon she thinks she's twenty-one. Independent, she is."

A clattering of footsteps on the stairs announced the subject of the conversation. Little Wanda skipped down the hallway and joyfully took Carmen's unbroken hand in hers. Her small freckled face tilted up to smile at the lady who needed her.

"You're here! I've been waiting for so long, and now you're finally here. We're going to have lots of fun, ma'am, and you're going to be all better here." She placed her small hand over Carmen's heart and looked in her eyes.

"Wanda Marie Bently!" Juanita Bently came out of the master-bedroom, linens stacked in her arms. "Let the lady be, at least until she's settled," she scolded, a shy smile lighting her freckled face.

Carmen noted the wild mane of red curls and freckles that stippled everywhere exposed skin showed. Smiling back, she decided she liked this young woman with the unusual golden eyes—eyes that radiated warmth and welcome.

"I'm Juanita. Sorry if she's pestering you, Ms. Fuentes. She's been saying a lady was coming for most of this month, and she couldn't wait for her to get here. Guess that's you? Don't know how she knows these things, but here you are." She smiled again, and looking over her shoulder she said, "Follow me, if you dare. Your room is next to Little Wanda's."

TWENTY-EIGHT

Chewing a piece of jerky, James Baytree washed it down with tepid water he'd gotten from the small pond nestled amidst a stand of willows. Hidden from view by the long strands of willow branches swaying in the afternoon breeze, he contemplated his next move.

Ultimately he figured he might lose the war, but his revenge would be costly to the folks of Hilldale, and to that stinking sheriff. Someone killed his boy, and he bet the law wouldn't so much as lift a finger to find out who did it. To them it was *good riddance to bad rubbish*. Well, his son wasn't garbage, and if he found out who took his boy's life, he'd make them pay, slow and painful.

His snitch in the hospital didn't know much, only that the boy died twitching and struggling like a frog on a hot griddle. Baytree ground his teeth. That lawyer woman was gonna die. He couldn't believe she survived the beatings and had gotten rescued. He'd make sure that didn't matter. She had to die. The sheriff had to die.

He went still. Not the sheriff. No, the sheriff had to live, his pregnant wife had to die. Her and their unborn kid. Eye-for-an-eye. He shivered in the afternoon heat. *I'm coming for your family, Sheriff. You're gonna hurt the way I'm hurting, and soon.*

He settled back against the trunk of the willow and thought about his plan, chuckling at the suffering he was going to dish out.

TWENTY-NINE

Little Wanda stood in the open doorway and watched the pretty lady staring out the bedroom window. She looked sad. Someone had hurt her real bad, and Little Wanda couldn't understand why folks did stuff like that to each other. She wished everyone had a Papa and Mama, and friends like hers.

But even if she was only seven, she knew sad. Knew how it hurt a person's heart. Grampa Billy died. That was her sad. Before he did, she'd gone to say goodbye to him, one last time. She had climbed on the bed ever so careful not to hurt his owies, and he had tried to smile. She felt joy knowing he knew she had come to see him.

She remembered his words after Miss Molly removed his oxygen mask. Words whispered so soft, she had to listen real careful to understand.

Little Wanda, you are a strong medicine woman and you must remember to be wise and loving with that gift. God is your source, never forget.

He'd coughed so hard she thought he wouldn't be able to finish telling her the rest of his words for her. Papa and Mama had wanted her to leave, wanted him to rest, but he'd waved them off, his hand so weak he could barely move it. He'd reached for hers and she'd held his tight. She hadn't been afraid because she knew where he was going, but she'd felt the sadness of knowing he had to leave her.

When you sing the healing song, when you pray, you let God's Spirit guide you. Never do it on your own, child.

He'd coughed some more. His voice so weak, she'd thought she should get down, but Grampa Billy wasn't finished, so she'd waited.

Nonhelema belongs to you, now. You must care for her gently, with great patience and love, you understand? Her wounds are deeper than her hide, so you must look beyond them and help her heart and mind heal. My time is short. Let me pray with you and then you must go.

Remembering, she watched the sad lady at the window and thought of Grampa Billy's prayer, and the last words he'd said about Nonhelema. She thought those words were for Miss Carmen, too.

THIRTY

Oscar Sumday sorted through the stack of papers on his father's small desk. The cabin's open doors and windows allowed the morning breeze to circulate the stale air, cooling the room to a tolerable temperature. Still, he wiped sweat from his brow.

He and his father had been on friendly terms for most of Oscar's adult life, but the unanswered questions still nagged and hurt. He'd never felt confident enough to ask them, and his father hadn't encouraged him to do so.

When Molly told him that Muley's parents had adopted his father, he'd been surprised, maybe a little hurt that his father had never shared that information with him. He'd always believed his father had been raised in foster care.

So many unanswered questions, the most painful of which was why had he left him with Mother Emma at the reservation all his growing up years? Why hadn't he kept his son, his only child, with him?

In one of the desk drawers he found a journal and paged through it. Here, as the sun warmed his back through the cabin window, he learned his great-grandfather, known as One-Who-Makes-True-Arrows, had gotten the name William Sumday because he refused to give a white-man's name to the registrar of the BIA before they would be allowed to receive their benefits of white flour crawling with weevils, and beef so rancid the dogs would barely eat it.

Each time he was told to choose a name, he would reply, *someday.* Frustrated, the registrar finally informed him he would now be known as William Sumday. Oscar read his father's words.

When the men came to take my father to the white man's school, and force my grandparents to leave Missouri, they asked my father's name. He only spoke Kickapoo and replied his name was One-Who-Talks-To-Horses. They laughed at him and told him his name would be the same as his father's.

When my parents were forced to flee and I was sent to a boarding school, I remembered my father's stories of his father. When asked my name, I replied, One-Who-Heals. Shaking their heads, they told me I would have my father's name. I can't remember my mother's or his face. It is all I have left of my father— his white man's name.

Oscar closed the journal and laid it with the items he wanted to keep. He continued to sort through the receipts and letters from the University where his father had taught before his wife died. After her death, he'd left the University, rarely returned to the reservation in Minnesota to visit him, and had built this cabin where he lived alone the rest of his life.

Shaking his head, Oscar stood and walked to his cooler, retrieved a cold bottle of water and the tuna sandwich his wife had made for him. Returning to the desk, he stared out the window at the stand of oaks and sycamore trees, wondering if his father had known loneliness, wondering if he'd ever missed his young son the way he'd missed his father.

He ate slowly, reluctant to finish his sorting and packing, wishing he could sweep it all away and head home.

Returning to his task while daylight made it possible to see, he reached to the back of the desk. There he found a metal cookie tin. Pulling it to the front, he pried it open and found several newspaper clippings. Oscar dumped them out and began reading the headlines.

A tingling heat crept up his body and rose to his face. They were the news articles of his mother's death, even a picture of himself, a three-year-old boy, eyes wide with fear and pain. Long suppressed memories flooded back.

Pain knifed through him. Dropping the newspaper clippings back into the tin, he closed the lid and laid it in the pile to take home. *Later*, he told himself. He'd go through them later.

THIRTY-ONE

Humming softly, Molly stood at her kitchen counter and spread mayonnaise on the slices of bread. Layering roasted chicken, Swiss cheese, dill pickles, and lettuce, she added the top slices and cut the sandwiches in half.

Footsteps on the porch made her quickly plate the lunch food and carry it to the table. Jedidiah, their Black and Tan hound, began a fierce barking from the back yard. Thinking he was as excited to see Dan as she was, she went to the back porch and tossed out a slice of chicken. The dog ignored the treat and continued to bark as he raced around the fenced in yard. Shrugging, Molly stepped back into the kitchen, closing the door.

The front screen door announced her husband's arrival in the house, and Molly smiled placing her hand over her abdomen. Before long they would be parents, and since her grandfather's passing, most days Dan ate his lunch at home, keeping an eye on her, trying to lift her spirits. She poured milk into glasses and set them next to their plates.

A sharp pain stabbed through her back and she tried to turn but a strong arm held her hard against a strange body. A body that was not her husband's.

Her baby leapt and turned, then lay still. Unable to comprehend the horrible pain, or know who was behind her, she tried to cry for help.

Struggling was useless and she stopped fearful of injuring her unborn son. *Help me, Lord! Save my baby,* her mind cried as her tears fell unchecked.

A foul-smelling hand covered her mouth and nose blocking her air. Fear flooded her. Praying Dan would get home soon, she once again tried to pull herself from her attacker's grasp.

"Ain't gonna make it," a voice rasped in her ear. Another stab of pain and she felt the warm rush of blood as it poured from her back, flooding down her legs. Her body trembled with shock, and she struggled to keep from fainting.

"Your man's gonna be home soon. This is for him." Strong, rough hands turned her and she came face-to-face with James Baytree. His eyes glittered with hatred, and his mouth twisted in a cruel smile.

"Welcome to hell." He released his grip on her arms, thrusting her backwards with a forceful shove. Unable to keep her balance, she felt herself falling.

Landing hard, her head struck the table and darkness swirled about her. As she sank into oblivion, she prayed God would protect her child.

THIRTY-TWO

Dan stepped into the kitchen. Calling out to Molly, he wondered at the silence that met him—except for Jedidiah. The hound howled with frustration as he tried to get through the back door. "Hang on," he called to the dog, "I'm coming to get you."

As he moved behind the center island, horror washed over him. Molly lay crumpled in a pool of blood, pale, unmoving. Rushing to her, he fell to his knees, and checked for her pulse, calling her name, whispering prayers.

Hands shaking, he dialed the office and instructed Vicki to get LifeFlite to their street. His voice trembling, he said, "She's lost a lot of blood, Vicki. Tell them to hurry, she's critical."

Pushing his phone back into his pocket, he retrieved kitchen towels and pressed them into the weeping wounds. Gently turning her over, he allowed her body weight to put pressure on the deep cuts, hoping to staunch the rapid flow.

Unconscious, Molly lay before him, and he felt helpless to save the woman and child he loved more than anything, or anyone, on earth. His hand buried in her hair, he prayed. As he waited for the sound of the medical helicopter, Dan's tears fell, streaming unchecked down his haggard face.

THIRTY-THREE

Carmen worked on stretching out her stiff muscles, and cautiously worked the injured ones, trying to get more mobility. The hot spray of the shower felt good, aiding in loosening the stiffness.

Hilldale Farewell

She could walk, though where her hip had been dislocated and the flesh around the hip joint badly bruised, caused her to limp. Grateful her legs weren't broken in the beatings, she determined to keep herself up and moving.

Forcing herself to work past the pain helped her focus on the present. She refused to think about the several days of captivity. Not yet.

She made her way down the stairs and stood in the kitchen doorway massaging the ache in her hip. Gordie, Juanita, and their daughter sat eating breakfast, the little girl chattering away, her parents responding with laughter and questions. Carmen wanted to run. Her heart twisted sending a sharp pain through her chest. She would never know what it was like to have a child. The pain swept through her leaving her nearly breathless.

Little Wanda looked up from her French toast and grinned at her. "Miss Carmen!" She jumped from her chair and skipped over to her. Taking her hand, she led Carmen to the chair next to hers.

"You get to sit by me," she gloated, as though she'd won a prize. "Ma made us French toast and bacon. It's so yummy! Hurry, 'cause I want you to meet Nonhelema, and Kissy, and Bossy. They've been waiting for you, too."

Climbing back in her chair, she commenced eating while Juanita took hot food from the oven and carried it to the table, placing it in front of Carmen. Smiling she said, "You're lucky there's anything left. I had to hide this to keep the food monster from getting it." Carmen smiled back and thanked her. Turning to the child next to her, she asked who the others were that were waiting for her.

Chewing rapidly, Little Wanda swallowed and said, "Did you know my Grampa Billy?" For a moment, her eyes held sadness.

"Nonhelema was his horse what got hurt when he did, but she's mine now. He gave her to me before he went to heaven. Nonhelema and me, we miss him." A single tear escaped and rolled down her freckled cheek.

Quickly swiping it away, she continued. "Kissy is Pa's milk cow 'cept she's pretty old now and don't give much milk. Bossy is her calf. She's going to have a baby of her own soon, then we can milk her." The child grinned at her. "Bossy is really bossy. Gotta watch out she don't push you around."

Carmen listened, shook her head trying to grasp all the information Little Wanda shared with her while trying to eat a bit of the food on her plate.

Billy Sumday. She had heard how Baytree's son had beaten him so severely, he'd died a few weeks later. Pushing her plate back, she nodded, trying not to allow the panic that threatened to have its way.

"I didn't know your grampa other than by sight," she answered. "I'm sorry he's gone, but I bet Nonhelema is happy to have you to take care of her. She won't be alone. Do you take care of all the animals?"

Little Wanda's golden eyes lit with joy. "I do mostly, but Pa has to help me with the heavy stuff. And Nonhelema and me, we're both happy. Grampa Billy told me I'm a healer woman and I've been singing the healing song and saying the healing prayers he taught me. Nonhelema is already doing better." Her chin came up and she looked in Carmen's eyes.

"I can sing the healing song for you, Miss Carmen. But you got to be ready, so I won't sing it today." Her child's voice held confidence and something else Carmen couldn't quite label.

Gordie smiled at his daughter. Reaching across the table, smoothing her wild red curls, he gently admonished her. "Let Miss Carmen be, Little Wanda. She may not want to go to the barn with you."

"No, that's okay, Mr. Bently, I was raised on a cattle ranch. I love animals," Carmen said. "I'd like to meet Nonhelema and the others. Besides, walking around outside will do me good. The sunshine looks inviting."

"Call me Gordie, please. Well, feel free to decline this little monkey's suggestions anytime you want to. She means no harm, and she loves the critters 'bout as much as she loves her Ma and me." His laugh was infectious. Carmen felt some of the heavy darkness that held her captive shift and lighten.

"She's not bothering me, and I'm grateful to be here. Please, don't worry about me." Looking at the child next to her, she continued, "I'm looking forward to spending time with her."

Pushing away from the table, she stood and got her balance. Little Wanda hopped from her chair and took her empty plate to the sink. She returned and looked up at Carmen. With the seriousness of one far older, she said, "You gotta eat more, Miss Carmen, 'cause you're gonna need it so you can help me with my chores."

"Wanda Marie Bently," her mother scolded, her forehead wrinkling in a frown. "Don't you go handing off your chores to Miss Carmen. Get on with you. Nonhelema's waiting for her breakfast, the cows need to get to the pasture, and your house chores will be right here when you get back."

Rolling her eyes, and with an exaggerated sigh, Little Wanda looked up at Carmen. "She always calls me by all my names when I'm in trouble. But you want to help me, right?" The child grinned up at her.

Hilldale Farewell

For the first time since her kidnapping, Carmen Fuentes laughed.

THIRTY-FOUR

Daniel Halloran paced the hospital hallway. Surrounded by friends and family, he couldn't look at them, couldn't speak to them. Trapped in his grief, his body and mind felt caged. Fear and rage tore at his mind as he tried to pray for his wife and unborn son. Surgeons were working to save them both, but Molly's condition was critical, and Dan couldn't bear the thought of losing the love of his life.

His deputies and U. S. Marshall Justin Taylor were scouring Hilldale and the surrounding area for Baytree, and Dan had given the order to bring him in, dead or alive.

He saw Oscar and Lydia Sumday whispering, Lydia's tears reminders of what had happened to their daughter—his wife. Had Dan not arrived minutes after the attack, Molly and their grandson would have died. Dan trembled at the thought.

Footsteps echoed down the hallway. All eyes turned to the weary surgeon making his way toward them, surgical mask dangling, a reminder of where he'd just come from. His voice was clear, but soft with sympathy for the waiting family. He pushed his hand through his hair and seemed surprised he still had on his surgical hat. Pulling it off, he looked from the parents to the husband of the woman he'd just operated on.

"We've done all we can. The rest is up to her. The baby appears to be fine, as far as we can tell, nearly seven pounds, and his lungs are working quite well." A tired smile tried to lighten the mood.

"Being a few weeks early, we were concerned about a couple of issues, but it appears his oxygen supply was adequate. The trauma of the attack, and the fall, seem not to have affected him. Mrs. Halloran may have wrapped her arms around her abdomen and fallen in such a way we could find no ill effects on, or in him. We'll keep him another day, just to make sure."

Dan felt tears start. "Molly, my wife, will she be okay?"

"Again, for now we've done all we can. She's somewhat stable, but she's lost a lot of blood, and that will take some time to recover from. We've given her four pints, and would be grateful for donations, if any of you have O positive?" Checking his watch, he continued.

"She'll be in ICU until we're sure she can breathe on her own and there's no bleeding where the knife entered. The right kidney had a small nick, but we believe it'll be fine, though only time will tell. It's miraculous she sustained no more serious injuries to her organs.

"If he continues to do well, the baby can go home tomorrow afternoon." Looking at Dan, and Molly's parents, he said, "I'm going to take you back to recovery even though she's not awake yet. You can sit with her a few minutes, let her hear your voices. I'm sorry we can't give you more information."

The solemn group headed down the hallway with Dan bringing up the rear. He wanted his time to be private. He understood her parents needed to see her, but when he talked to his wife, he wanted her to himself.

Clenching his fist, darkness filled Dan's mind. Prayers fell silent. Where was God in this nightmare? Rage seeped stealthily like a dank fog, filling his heart.

He promised himself that James Baytree would pay for all he'd done, and he hoped he would be the one to find him. He had a little business to attend to with him, and he didn't want witnesses.

THIRTY-FIVE

Juanita hung the last sheet on the clothesline, and as it flapped gently in the light breeze, she clipped the clothespins in place. Reaching in the basket for bath towels, she looked up at the woman standing beside her.

Carmen looked shy. "Would you like some help? It's been ages since I saw clothes hanging on a line. I love the smell when they dry outside.

"Mom used to hang her clothes out when I was a kid. One of the last memories I have of her was handing her towels from the basket. I was four." She stood waiting for Juanita's answer.

Almost refusing the help, Juanita realized this was the injured woman's way of reaching out. Handing over the towels and pointing to the hand-made clothespin bag, she smiled. "I'd love some help. I'd never hung up clothes in my life until I married Gordie and moved here to the farm. It's such a wonderful exercise in so many ways, and it's free energy."

Carmen struggled to lift her casted broken arm. Embarrassed, she realized she couldn't reach the clothesline. Juanita took the towels and said, "I'm so sorry. I wasn't thinking."

"It's okay," Carmen shrugged trying to pretend it didn't matter. "Please, don't feel bad."

Juanita nodded and smiled, grateful that Carmen stayed.

"Well, we tell Little Wanda about cooperation, guess we should try it ourselves! How about you hand me clothespins, and we can visit while I finish up. It's such a beautiful morning, we can't let it go to waste, can we?"

Nodding, Carmen scooped the wooden pegs from the bag fashioned from the trunk of a pair of old jeans, and held them out to the young woman.

"Your daughter is charming. She's so full of life and seems so confident. You and Gordie are great parents. Her laugh sounds like her father's, but she's got your looks." Smiling, Carmen thought of the friendly evening visits Little Wanda made to her room before bedtime. "She's certainly a smart little girl."

Juanita finished hanging up the towels, and Carmen tossed the extra pins back in the bag. Juanita picked up the laundry basket. "Let's sit on the porch a bit. Iced tea?" Carmen nodded and the two headed for the house.

Settled into wicker rockers with their tea, Juanita stared out to the barn and the fields beyond. She loved this farm, it's peacefulness and country beauty.

"It's like heaven for me here. I grew up in a dumpy apartment in Minneapolis and had no idea this life would ever be mine.

"My mom died when I was seventeen, and I ran away to find my grandparents here in Hilldale."

She glanced at Carmen quietly rocking and sipping her tea. "I was already pregnant with Little Wanda, and I'm blessed I didn't lose her on the way down south. I walked and hitchhiked. It took me almost a month and I can tell you, I got awfully hungry. It's a miracle she was born safe and sound."

Juanita sipped her tea and set the sweating glass on the table between them. Looking at the woman next to her, she thought about her next words. Rarely did she talk about that time in her life, but something in her knew it was time to share some of it with this broken woman whom God had sent into their lives.

"Little Wanda is a product of rape. My mother was an addict and an alcoholic. Her boy friends thought I was part of a package deal. A few gave me these." She pulled up her sleeves and exposed crude tattoos crawling up her freckled arms.

"The last one got me pregnant, though I didn't realize it at first. When Mom overdosed, I knew I couldn't stay in the apartment, and juvenal hall or foster care weren't an option for me. I ran away."

Shrugging, she stared out to the gravel road and beyond, to the field of corn rustling in the morning breeze. "I'd heard my grandparents had a farm in Hilldale, Missouri. I thought if I could make it there, my Mom's boyfriend wouldn't find me, and my grandparents would take me in. I'd be home.

"The guy found me. Kidnapped another girl and me, nearly killed us both." Juanita's eyes grew dark as wildflower honey with the memory.

"The house where we were held caught fire. Little Wanda picked that time to be born and I delivered her in the bathtub, fire all around us. I didn't know if we'd get out alive. Then, there was Gordie. Came through those flames and rescued Little Wanda and me. Saved the other girl."

Carmen looked at her. "How could you keep her—the baby? And your husband doesn't mind?" Shaking her head and at a loss for words, she took another drink of her tea.

Laughing, Juanita replied, "Gordie didn't give me much of a choice. He knew she was going to be a girl before any of the rest of us, and he kept after me about taking care of us. I called her *it* and he scolded me to give her a name, and to love her. He offered to marry me in name only, so she'd have a name and a daddy. He wouldn't hardly take *no* for an answer."

She looked at Carmen, a blush sweeping across her cheeks. "I grew to love him, with his kindness, his gentle ways. He never asked for anything except to be part of the baby's life.

"There's lots of news articles on Gordie's life before we met. You may want to look them up sometime, read them. He's an amazing man. My life was nothing compared to what he survived."

Uncomfortable with the direction of the conversation, Carmen stood. "I think I'll go lie down for awhile. I'm sorry about your life, and the bad times, but that daughter of yours is certainly a gift. You and your husband are amazing people, and I doubt that I would have been as good as the two of you. Thank you for sharing your story."

Juanita heard her haltering steps labor up the stairs. Leaning back in her rocker, she took up her tea and drank, letting the icy liquid clear the lump in her throat.

THIRTY-SIX

"Heard Molly's home. Sure glad she's recovering good, and your boy is okay." Randy Carter entered the breakroom with a container of cupcakes. Setting them on the counter, he removed the lid and looked them over. "You calling him Will? Billy?"

"Billy," Dan replied, pouring Randy a cup of coffee before putting the pot back on the hot plate. "Doctor says Molly's got to take it easy, not pop her stitches. Her folks kept Billy at their place until she arrived home. Lydia's staying with us for a few weeks, to help out." He eyed the cupcakes.

Randy picked up his cup of coffee and took a cautious taste. He added cold water to the brew before setting it back on the counter.

"Couple of hunters found an abandoned camp. It's rough and they thought it might be Baytree's." He reached for a chocolate cupcake with sprinkles. He sure loved those sprinkles, and his wife knew that.

Hilldale Farewell

Peeling off the paper wrapper, he took a bite and waited for Dan. Heading back to the sheriff's office, the two men passed Vicki's desk and saluted.

Baker, receptionist, dispatcher, and Randy's wife, they wanted to show their appreciation for the goodies. Blowing her a kiss, Randy followed his boss.

"Where'd they see this camp?" The sheriff settled in his chair, took a bite of cupcake, and picked up his mug of coffee. His eyes on his deputy, he blew across the steaming surface and took a sip.

"Off Hawkins road. That timber back of old man Hawkins pasture. There's a clearing with a small pond surrounded by willows. Looks like he stayed a day or two. No fire. Left a few empty tins, and looks like he might of took sick."

Dan locked eyes with Randy. "Took sick? How do you reckon they know that?"

"Found some of his—umm—scat. Looked bloody."

Leaning back in his chair, Dan finished his cupcake and licked the icing from his fingers. "I'll go look around. You and Jeff interview the hunters, get their statements. I'll see what I can find at the campsite. Might not be him. Not much way to know."

Nodding, Randy made to leave then turned back. "Could take that Texas fella with you. He's a tracker. Could be he'd catch a trail. Reckon between the two of you, you'd be able to follow it, even if it's a few days gone." Dan sipped his coffee, not answering. Shrugging, Randy left the office to find Jeff.

Eyes opaque, mouth set in a grim line, the sheriff left his mug on his desk and stood, checked his gun, took his Stetson from the rack, and headed out to the parking lot. He didn't want anyone with him, just in case he found James Baytree.

THIRTY-SEVEN

Carmen wandered out to the barn in search of Little Wanda. Focusing on walking without a limp, she tried not to favor her bruised hip. No good. Still tender, she slowed her steps and eased the weight to her good hip.

She found the little girl standing on a stool brushing Nonhelema. "Well, here I am. You said you needed help?" The mare nuzzled the child, nearly knocking her off her perch.

"Whoa," Little Wanda laughed, patting the head pushing against her. "I love you, too!"

Turning to Carmen she grinned. "That's Nonhelema's way of showing she loves me. But she's big and strong, and sometimes she knocks me down. She doesn't mean to hurt me, she just hasn't learned I'm a kid warrior, and she's a grown-up warrior. And yes, I would love to have help." Mischief lit her eyes. "Did you tell my Ma you were helping me with my chores?"

"Warrior? Oh, and no on the telling your mom. She and your father are working the fence line. Seems Bossy got out and they're trying to find out where the break is."

The child intrigued Carmen. Her poise, intelligence, and self-confidence, the sincere knowledge, without arrogance, that she was loved. The little girl's ability to show love to those around her, including Carmen, amazed her.

"Really, Ma won't care, but she doesn't want me to bug you, at least not too much." Eyeing Carmen, she asked, "Am I? You know, bugging you too much?"

Shaking her head, Carmen smiled. "Not yet. Now tell me about this warrior business." Little Wanda grinned and nodded.

"Nonhelema is named after a Shawnee warrior woman. Grampa Billy said she was the chief of her tribe. Not many women get to be chief, you know.

"Nonhelema fought for Grampa Billy, got hurt real bad, and my grampa died. But if she didn't fight the bad guys, Grampa wouldn't have been able to say the blessing over Little Billy, and never could have told me about being a medicine woman, and pray his blessing over me." Shrugging her shoulders, she looked sad. "Sometimes it hurts to be a warrior."

Her golden eyes settled on Carmen. Handing her the curry brush, she watched the woman work the horse's flank. Unable to use her broken arm, Little Wanda wondered if the lady would quit. But she didn't and Little Wanda nodded to herself. So far so good!

Seeing her helper knew what she was doing, she hopped from her stool to retrieve a curry comb to work hay from the mane.

Returning to her perch, she began to ease the comb through the long brown and black strands of coarse hair, plucking straw and hay from the comb.

"You know, I'm kinda a warrior. I fight sickness and owies." Looking up at Carmen, she continued. "You're kinda a warrior, too. Pa said you fight bad people and try to get justice for the good ones. Not sure what justice is, but I think it's like time out."

Carmen stopped brushing. "Time out?"

"Yeah, time out. I get time out when I'm naughty. I'm supposed to think about what I did, and feel sorry so I won't do it again. Sometimes I forget and think about riding Nonhelema, or walking in the woods with the dogs. But time out, I think, is kind of what justice is like. You get the bad guys put in time out, right?"

Hilldale Farewell

Not wanting to try to explain that a public defender often must defend bad guys, Carmen let the question rest. But the child's words opened a door in her mind. She realized she would never go back to being a public defender, no matter how righteous it first seemed. James Baytree should never be set free, and she never wanted to defend someone like him again.

"That's as good a description of justice I've ever heard, Little Wanda." She wanted to change the subject.

"How's this look? Think I can start on the other side?" Grinning, she watched as the girl examined her grooming job. Pronouncing it well done, she gave permission for Carmen to continue to the mare's other side, gently drawing her hand across the horse's flank to keep her from startling and kicking out.

"You've done this before, haven't you?" Little Wanda raised on her tippy-toes to look at her helper over Nonhelema's back.

"I have," admitted Carmen. "My father and I lived on a big cattle ranch in Texas, and I've been working and riding horses since I was five. I love everything about horses."

And it was true. Carmen realized that the smell, the feel, the sounds of the barn, of being around the mare brought her precious moments of peace where she forgot her anger, her sorrow, her fear. Her losses shrank, and healing began to fill the dark, empty places. She wished to hug the child for pushing her into helping her with her chores, but still felt a bit awkward with the simple physical manifestation of her emotions.

Did Little Wanda somehow know this was perfect medicine for her? She looked up and saw the little freckled face giving her a cheeky grin. Carmen laughed out loud.

THIRTY-EIGHT

Muley Burger sat at his kitchen table across from Gordie and Juanita. Concern lit the young couple's faces, and he hoped he could make them understand why he wanted to move to town.

Six years ago, he'd purchased Obed Martin's house. His old friend had passed away saving Juanita's life, and Muley couldn't let the house go to strangers. When Obed's son decided to sell the house, he'd snapped it up. After fixing it, he'd rented it out, content to stay at the farm.

Now, all this business with Billy's murder, Neely's Café getting blown to smithereens, Molly Halloran getting knifed in her very own kitchen, why he wanted to be in town, help Danny watch after their loved ones.

Besides, he'd be living right across from Miss Mary Harmon and Juanita's grandma, Wanda Harmon. Both could cook, both grew up with the same folks he did, and he sure enough enjoyed the many hours they spent visiting over meals nearly as good as his Emily used to make.

After Baytree's attack on Molly, he fretted about his two friends being alone and felt he was just the man to take on the job of protecting them. Now to convince the youngsters that it weren't their fault, his leaving. He just knew it was the right thing for him to do.

"Don't go looking like a hound what lost his coon," he grinned at Gordie. "I can still drive as far as the farm and back, and I'll visit enough you'll be right happy I got a place to go home to."

"If you're sure you're good with this, we'll back you all the way, Papa Muley," Gordie said, studying his dear friend's face. "You know we love you, and you've always got a home with us. Hope we ain't run you off with helping Miss Carmen, and all. Has Little Wanda got you wore out with her shenanigans?"

"Land sakes, no!" Muley took a deep drink of his sweet tea. Smiling at Juanita, he said, "Sure did learn how to make sweet tea, young lady. Best tea next to my Emily's." Juanita blushed and smiled back.

"Now," he continued, "If'n you kids will give me a hand, I ain't planning on taking much but my personal stuff, and a few of Emily's pretties. Most things I'll leave for you, Juanita. She'd be right proud of how you've taken to the farm and all. Reckon she'd see you as a daughter to her." His voice cracked and he cleared his throat.

"I'm headed to clean out my room, and sure could use help with the laundry I stored up when Billy lay abed in the hospital." Again, his voice caught and he shook his head.

"Reckon I'm getting sentimental in my old age. How 'bout we get a load moved today, and I'll stay at the house in town tonight. Don't like leaving the ladies too long unprotected."

Grinning, Gordie finished his tea, chewed a chunk of ice, and stood. "Got some boxes in the storage room I was fixing to haul off. Reckon we can put them to good use."

While Juanita cleared the table, the men headed off to get Muley started on a new life in town.

THIRTY-NINE

She woke wet with night-sweats. Fear rampaged through her setting her body on fire. Trying to get out of bed without waking Danny, Molly stood, trembling with the vestiges of her nightmare.

Hilldale Farewell

Billy slept peacefully in the bassinet next to her bed. Laying her hand on his tummy, she felt its gentle rhythm as her tiny son slept peacefully. Molly moved her hand to his head, stroking his silky dark curls. Billy sighed, brought his tiny fist to his mouth, and slept on.

Satisfied her son was fine, and knowing his father slept close by, she padded into the kitchen. The nightlight sent shadows skittering across the room. Stopping in the doorway to check that no one lay in wait for her, she checked the door locks again before she continued into the kitchen. She lit the gas burner beneath the tea pot, took her favorite mug from the rack over the sink, and plunked a tea bag inside. No more sleep tonight.

As she sipped her chamomile tea, she stared at the floor. Her mother had scrubbed the tiles until they were spotless, and though she'd never seen anything but the crime scene photos, Molly still saw the pool of her blood, still felt the heat of it as it ran down her back and legs. Still felt the fear that her unborn child had been injured, or killed, in the attack.

She willed herself to sip tea and focus on being grateful Billy survived unscathed, and she was healing—at least her body was. Nightmares still ruled her sleep. Footsteps on the porch still sent her heart into overdrive. Even locking the doors—something they had never done before—fear swept her up at the tiniest reminder.

A dark shadow filled the doorway and her heart skipped a beat. She knew it was not *him,* but she couldn't stop the involuntary cry before it escaped. Her husband walked to the table and sat, taking her clutched fist in his warm hand, gently unfolding her fingers, kissing her palm.

"It's okay, Molly. It's okay to be scared. You've been through a terrible attack and it'll take time to work through it. Don't beat yourself up over your fear. Give yourself time."

Molly swiped at her tears. "Billy needs a mother who isn't tired from being up half the night, who isn't afraid of her own shadow!"

"Hey, sweet lady," Dan brought his face close to hers, studying her turbulent green eyes. "You are getting better. You came in here in the dark, by yourself, made tea, you're sitting here not screaming. You are doing better."

"I'm getting better at hiding my fear, Danny." Molly felt the welcome warmth of his hand gently squeezing hers. She loved this man. Loved him more than her life, and she wanted to be well, to be whole for him, for their new-born son. Shaking her head, she leaned across the short expanse between them and kissed her husband. Dan returned her kiss.

"Remember what your grandfather told you?"

Molly stared at him. In her fear and depression, she'd almost forgotten his words about their baby's future. Closing her eyes, she thought a moment before she repeated them.

"I love you, Granddaughter. Rough water's ahead, but trust that rescue is sure. Your son will touch many hearts and bring peace to many troubled minds. Do not waver from your faith, child, for God is faithful to bring you through the fire. Forgive, that you be forgiven. You and your love have been a blessing to me."

Smiling through her tears, she squeezed her husband's hand. "I love you, Danny Halloran. You and Billy are the best gift that I've ever received, and I know I am truly blessed. I will get better. Pray with me?"

The two sat holding hands, Dan praying quietly, pouring out the love and gratitude he felt for his little family. Neither saw Lydia Sumday tiptoe from the kitchen doorway back to the guest room.

FORTY

September skies swept across the Mid-Missouri country-side. Manuel Fuentes drove his pickup along the gravel road back to the highway. Headed for Hilldale, the lovely scenes of ripening fields were lost to him. He'd just visited his daughter at the Burger farm and felt relieved at the improvements he'd seen in her, both physically and mentally, but, she was far from being healed. His fists clenched the steering wheel.

Her beautiful dark eyes were still filled with shadows, dark and haunted, and she'd instinctively stiffened and winced when he'd hugged her, apologizing with tears. His heart ached for her and he felt angry that he couldn't fix the wrongs done to her.

Fury simmered deep and hot in his belly. He must find this Baytree man and punish him for what he'd taken from his beloved Carmen.

FORTY-ONE

He vomited hard. Soiling himself, James Baytree backed against a sycamore shivering in the shade. Trying to focus on his surroundings, he thought he heard twigs snap, a faint rustling of ground cover. Pain twisted his gut and he groaned.

"Hands up!" The voice, harsh and cold, brought Baytree's head up. His stomach roiled signaling another round of heaving. Ignoring the command, he leaned over again. Dry heaves racked his body. When the spasms abated, he looked up at the man standing before him.

"Shoot me. I ain't going nowhere with you," he growled, wiping his mouth on his tattered, filthy shirt.

"Fine with me. Nothing I'd like better." U. S. Marshall Justin Taylor held his revolver steady.

"You're under arrest for the murder of William Sumday, the kidnapping, beating, and rape of Carmen Fuentes, and the bombing—," before he could finish Baytree threw a fist full of debris in his face and moved to tackle him, thrusting his head and shoulder into Justin's chest.

Grunting at the blow and shaking dirt from his eyes, he brought the butt of his gun down hard on Baytree's head. Cursing, the prisoner dropped to the ground.

The U. S. Marshall stood over him. Holstering his weapon, he grabbed the writhing man with one hand and cocked his fist with the other. Yanking him to his feet, he snarled, "You are a dead man, Baytree. You understand? A dead man."

"Let him go, Justin."

Still clutching Baytree by his shirt, Justin turned to where Sheriff Dan Halloran stood, face dark and still, his hand resting on the holstered pistol grip of his gun.

"I said let him go. This is my jurisdiction, my prisoner. You get on back to the office and file your report. I'll bring him in, assuming he doesn't give me any trouble."

Justin stared at Dan. The sheriff's voice was soft and deadly, his eyes opaque with anger. Realizing what the sheriff may have in mind, the U. S. Marshall cleared his throat, and shook his head.

"I expect we should both be taking him in, Sheriff. Look Dan, I know what it looks like, but I wasn't going to kill him—just rough him up some. He'll spend the rest of his life in prison, that's good enough for me."

Dan stared him down. "That's bull, and you know it. Spending the rest of his life in prison isn't good enough for what he did to Ms. Fuentes, to my wife and son, to Billy Sumday. You need to leave. This is on me."

He stared at Justin. Again, the Marshall saw the intent in Dan's eyes and shook his head. "Can't let you do that, Dan. You're too good a lawman, too good a man. You do what I'm thinking you're thinking, who's going to look after your wife and son?

"I admit, I planned on roughing him up a bit, but look at him. He's half dead. He smells like a sewer, and needs to get to a hospital before he can't stand trial and pay for what he's done to Hilldale." His fist still firmly twisted in Baytree's filthy shirt, Justin shook the man like a dog shaking a rat.

"No fight in him. Wouldn't be fair. Wouldn't be satisfactory, Dan. Besides, much as I dislike it, revenge isn't ours." His mouth closed in a hard line.

Before he knew what happened, Dan's fist flew. Justin jerked his head to the side and heard the rush of air as the blow flew by his ear. Shoving

Baytree to the ground, he whirled just in time to block the next strike. Grabbing Dan's arm, he twisted it back and braced his leg against the furious sheriff's knee, dropping him to the ground.

Dan leapt to his feet, fists cocked. The sound of their ragged breathing filled the area around them. Baytree, in a huddle on the ground nearby, barked out a laugh, startling both men.

"Fighting the wrong man, Dan," Justin said, his voice quiet but firm.

Dan's body went still. His eyes never leaving Justin's face, he saw the Marshall wasn't backing off. Anger warred with what he knew was right. The need to hurt the man on the ground the way he hurt Molly, and all the folks of Hilldale, rode him like hives on a hot day, but Justin was right. That realization didn't make the surrender of his anger any easier. Lowering his fists, he gritted his teeth.

"You're right. I'll call the University Hospital and give them a heads-up. We can take my vehicle, come back for yours later."

Shaking his head, Dan wiped his hand across his face, as though wiping the cobwebs of hate away. "I owe you for that, Justin. Someday I might even thank you. How'd you beat me to finding him?"

The U. S. Marshall grinned. "I'm an excellent tracker, remember?" His grin disappeared, replaced by a frown. "You don't owe me anything, Dan. No more than I owe you for showing up when you did. My original intent wasn't much better, but he isn't worth losing the life we have. I need to be there for Carmen, you need to be there for your family, for your town. Let's get this dirt-bag to the hospital."

The two men escorted Baytree, half-carrying him in his weakened state. Once ensconced in the back of Dan's vehicle, Baytree slipped into unconsciousness. The two men drove in silence, both lost in thoughts of what they'd almost done.

FORTY-TWO

Carmen leaned back in Muley's recliner. Afternoon shadows stretched across the living room and she watched their progress, feeling as though they were reaching out to her with their soft, dark comfort—comfort she refused to accept, no matter where it came from.

She wasn't sleeping well, and knowing that Justin was waiting for an answer about returning to Texas with him, had her awake in her room most of the night.

Tired, soul-weary, unable to cry or grieve for herself, anger and despair ruled her thoughts. Her eyes, blood-shot and red-rimmed, glared at him. Justin sat across from her, waiting.

"I'm unable to have children," she whispered, voice hoarse with emotion. "I'm badly scarred, and

I'll have permanent disfigurement. It will take many plastic surgeries to repair some—Did you hear me, Justin?—*some* of the damage done to my face. My body will never work the same again. Still blocking out the mental and emotional baggage I must come to grips with—baggage I'll probably carry for the rest of my life.

"You are looking at a woman who should be dead. Who would be better off dead."

She pulled her eyes from his face and stared at the floor, her hands trembling even as she clasped them in her lap. Heat flared across her cheeks and she cleared her throat, but her voice still rang with her pain.

"Go away, Justin. Just get up and walk out that door, head back to Texas and don't come back. That's what's best for both of us." Defeat road her shoulders, dulled her once snapping-black eyes. "Go away," she repeated.

Justin leaned back in his chair and studied her face. He wanted to weep, to yell, to bust up the furniture, but instead, he took a deep breath and blew it out.

"Well, when I asked you to come back home with me, your answer left no room for doubt." Carmen's head lifted and her eyes met his. A smile tugged at the corner of his lips.

"Are you laughing at me, Justin Paul Taylor? So help me…" For just an instant, fire flashed from her eyes before it faded away.

"No!" he sighed, the hint of smile gone. "No, it's just nice to see that spark of fierceness, of fighting back." He wanted to touch her hand, to touch her hair, trace the scars on her face, but knew better. Too soon.

"Anything else you want to say? I believe it's my turn?" Leaning toward her, he tried to carefully choose his words—not his best attribute. He prayed his love for her would shine through.

Her emotions danced between despair, anger, confusion, fear, back to despair. He saw it all in her eyes, her battered face. And he loved her even more.

"Okay. So, you can't have babies. If the man you loved became sterile, would you dump him? Uh-uh," he wagged his finger at her as she began to answer. "Rhetorical question, because I know the answer. My turn, remember?" He really wanted to kiss her.

"You wouldn't. You would name all the reasons why it wouldn't matter to you, to your relationship. And rightfully so." He raked his fingers through his hair.

"Of course it will alter some things, but never the love we have for one another. God will provide a child, if we are to have a child in our lives. Whether it's fostering, adoption, or a basket on the doorstep, it doesn't matter, Carmen. God will work out the details." Again, he studied her face, her eyes.

"The rest of you—it's the wrapping on a gift. You are a gift, always have been since the first day you punched me in the barn lot, knocking me into the manure.

"I'm sorry about all the damage done to you, and believe me, that man will pay for what he did. I can't fix or change what's happened. I can love you through the surgeries, through whatever life throws at us, no matter what. If I wanted to quit loving you, I'd have done it when you left Texas a year ago. You are part of me, and I believe and hope I'm part of you."

A sound much like a strangled sob erupted from Carmen's throat. Shaking her head, her hands fisted on her knees, she ground out, "I'm damaged, all right. Soiled. Spoiled goods. Every time you touched me you'd think of that. I know you would. And I would, as well. I don't know if I'll ever be able to love the way a wife should." A heavy sigh escaped, and her fists struck her thighs.

"I will never be good enough. Never, Justin."

His eyebrows drew together. "You must take me for a fool, or a very shallow man, if you really believe that. I don't think you believe that of me, but I do think that's what you believe of yourself. I'm willing to wait, but I want to be around you, love you, help you heal." He shrugged.

"You're wrong about not being good enough. You were created for me. The person you are inside and out. God doesn't make mistakes—"

This time she didn't allow him to finish. Shouting, her breath coming in ragged gasps, she raged, "God doesn't make mistakes? GOD DOESN'T MAKE MISTAKES? Look at me. What happened to me was by His design? What kind of father allows his daughter to be beaten nearly to death, and repeatedly raped? He could have saved me. He could have protected me from those animals. Where was God then? Where was He?"

Justin sat silent. Here was the truth of her wounded spirit. She believed God didn't care that she'd been savaged, that He'd just stood by and let it happen. How could he answer her?

He'd raged night after night at God, asking the same questions. And he didn't know the answers. He just knew that God loved them, was for them, not against them, was for their construction, not their destruction.

"Carmen, I don't have the answers to that. But I know this beyond a shadow of a doubt, God was right there with you, suffering with you. I believe He never left you, and I believe he led me straight to you." He locked eyes with her. "I knew where to find you. That was God, by His Holy Spirit leading me.

"Good enough? None of us are good enough no matter what we look like, or act like. We're all flawed. Some flaws just show more than others. But listen to me. If you get nothing else of what I'm trying to say, get this," his voice hushed as awe overwhelmed him.

"You, Carmen Maria Fuentes are good enough that a king died for you. Was beaten, and tortured, and hung on a cross for you. For me."

Carmen stared at him, mouth open to refute his words. Nothing came out. She tried. Words formed, she tried to utter them, but still, silence reigned.

Justin feared he'd pushed her too far. Said too much. As he searched her face, he saw the conflicting emotions racing, colliding, hurting.

And then she wept.

Sobs, deep and harsh, ripped from her. Tears rolled, and pooled, and soaked her face, ravaged by the brutal blows of a madman. Rage tore through her and poured forth in cries that only one wounded so terribly could utter. And still she wept. Justin dropped to his knees before her and silently asked permission to hold her.

Ignoring her casts, her bandages, she slid from the recliner and would have landed hard, but his hands caught her, pulled her against him, cradling her gently but firmly to his chest.

Her fists flailed against him. He didn't stop them because he knew the blows weren't directed at him, but at the monsters who'd tried to destroy her.

He had no idea the words he murmured in her ear, only that he wanted to pour his love and desire to comfort her, into her anguished heart and mind. He prayed she would find peace in his arms, in the beating of his heart as it rode the tide of pain with her.

He held her as the shadows deepened across the farm and the sounds of life crept back into the house. The screen door closing, the laughter of Little Wanda, the voices of her parents returning from the barn. Life in the midst of the storm.

He held her as her sobs ebbed and flowed, and finally quieted. He held her as she lay spent in his arms. He held her firm against him, knowing how her shattered world threatened to fly apart, scattering the pieces, leaving her permanently broken.

With his love, prayers, and his gentle embrace, Justin did his best to hold those pieces together, until she grew strong enough to do it for herself.

FORTY-THREE

Molly listened to Dan. Horror widened her eyes and paled her skin. "He's in the hospital? You've got him and he's in the hospital?"

Nodding, Dan pulled her into his arms, holding her trembling body. "He's not going anywhere. I've ordered the hospital to keep a guard posted 24/7, outside his door. No one enters or leaves without the guard checking. Soon as he's fit to stand trial Baytree's going to jail for the rest of his life. It's over, my love. It's over."

"Not until he's off in prison somewhere away from here. He killed Grampa and nearly killed our son. He should have died in those woods, Danny." Bitterness sharpened her voice, and Dan felt her hot tears as they soaked his shirt.

"Don't let hate for him take over, Molly. He'll win with his evil ways if you let hate have its way in your heart. If it wasn't for Justin, I'd have done something stupid—or worse—out there. Could have lost my job and my freedom." His voice shook as his arms tightened around her. "I could have lost you and Billy."

Dan led Molly to a chair and pulled her down on his lap. Wrapping his arms around her, he held her against him, letting his words sink in. Feeling her in his arms, knowing what he'd almost thrown away by allowing hatred and anger to rule, he swallowed hard.

"Don't let hate win, Molly," he repeated softly in her ear. "God and the law will deal with James Baytree." He held his wife until her tears stopped and she slept, her head on his shoulder. Lifting her, he carried her to the bedroom and put her on their bed. Billy, asleep, sucked on his pacifier. Molly sighed in her sleep. Covering her, Dan looked at the two people he loved most in the world.

"Please God, don't ever let me compromise my faith and love again. Too high a cost," he whispered. "Too high a cost."

FORTY-FOUR

James Baytree lay cuffed to the hospital bed. He looked around the room, tried the cuffs and found they held. Cursing, he closed his eyes. He had so many more plans to carry out, and here he was, caught like a coyote in a trap.

The guard posted outside his door saw he was awake, pulled his cell phone from his pocket and made a call, watching him through the window as he talked. *Company's comin',* Baytree thought.

Pushing his button to summon the nurse, he waited. He watched as the guard checked the nurse's ID before letting her in. Recognizing her, Baytree laughed. If his plan worked, he'd be out of this joint within a few minutes. Idiots didn't realize just how determined he was to destroy them. They'd learn, he promised himself. They'd learn.

"Can I help you?" the nurse asked, moving to his bed, blocking the view of the guard.

"Need to use the toilet, sweetheart."

The nurse motioned for the guard and explained the situation. "Use the bedpan," the guard growled, "I'm not unlocking the cuffs."

Nodding, the nurse moved behind the guard, but instead of getting the bedpan, she jabbed a needle into his exposed neck, depressing the plunger on the syringe. Almost instantly, he sank to the floor.

"Atta girl." James Baytree grinned. "Knew I could count on you, Roxy. Get me out of here, I got work to do."

Roxanne Blythe rifled through the unconscious guard's pockets, retrieved the key, and released the cuffs. Baytree climbed out of bed pulling the IV needle from his arm. "Clothes?"

"I stored them in the closet." Handing him a bottle of tablets, she instructed him, "Take one of these twice a day. There's a backpack behind the dumpster in the alley with food, water, and a change of clothes." Reaching her hand out, she patted his cheek. He batted her hand away.

Roxanne pulled back her cheeks flushing. She started to reach for him again and stopped her hand in mid-air. Sighing, she spoke softly, urgently, her eyes pleading with him.

"Don't hurt anyone else, Jimmy, please. You payed them back enough. That sheriff's baby could have died. He's innocent of any wrong-doing. You made them pay for Macon, now just get out of here and head to Mexico, or Canada. I put enough cash in the backpack to get you far away from here."

Quickly, before he could resist, she hugged her step-brother, then turned and walked from the room. Heavy sadness for James, and for herself, weighed her heart down. She hurried down the hall. She wouldn't let him see her tears.

FORTY-FIVE

Dan looked around the table at the men eating, sipping from mugs of steaming coffee. Breakfast at Dotty's Café meant good food, good service, and good company. But he had an agenda this morning. He'd invited Carter Neely to join Muley Burger, and John Ed Sapp, owner of Sapp's Construction.

Dotty Mann, owner and cook, grinned down at Carter. "Well, Mr. Neely, does the food pass inspection?" She refilled his mug and reached toward John Ed's. "Sure sorry to hear about your café."

She set the pot on the table and reached into her apron pocket. "We took up a collection and raised a little money to help you get rebuilt. Thursday night is music night and we're doing a benefit for your place. Maybe you and Tina would like to stop by?"

Carter looked at the generous amount written on the check in his hand. "I'd be honored, Dotty," he said. "Thanks for this. Wasn't sure I wanted to rebuild, but reckon this kinda makes the decision for us."

John Ed reached into his shirt pocket and pulled out another check. "My brother, Billy Jack, ate at your place every morning he could. Sure misses it, and insisted the company make a donation. Dan hauled us here to Dotty's to seal the deal!"

Stunned, Carter stammered and wiped at his eyes. Muley Burger laughed and slapped another check on the table. "Ain't letting you off that easy, boy. Reckon you got our money, now you got to get to rebuilding.

"John Ed says his company can do the main building for the insurance money, but this here money is for outfitting the place and getting the show on the road. Much as I like Dotty's, Hartsburg is a bit far for me to drive anymore. 'Sides, rumor has it she's thinking she's got to retire and get into all kind of trouble with them there sisters of hers."

Looking around the table, Carter said, "This is totally unexpected. Don't know how to thank you all, except to convince Tina we're going back into business. And Dotty," he reached out and took her hand, "this means more than I can say. It's folks like you all that make life worth living. Thank you."

Patting his shoulder, Dotty retrieved her coffee pot and headed back to the counter. "You're welcome, my friend. See you Thursday night. Oh, and when you get ready to outfit your place, come see me. Got plenty to sell when that rumor comes true."

The men finished their breakfast and piled into their respective vehicles. Dan waited until Muley and Carter buckled up, then headed home to Hilldale, each man deep into their own thoughts of the morning events.

The sheriff dropped the men at their homes and headed to his office. His cell phone buzzed and pulling it from his pocket, he listened as Vicki informed him of James Baytree's escape from the hospital.

The peace of the morning turned to a knot in his stomach. He knew this wasn't going to end well—not for any of them.

FORTY-SIX

Baytree wasted no time in stealing what he needed to create another crude bomb. As he assembled it, he mumbled to himself, cursing the town of Hilldale and its inhabitants.

He felt no remorse taking his step-sister's money and using it to further his revenge. She had always been a sucker for his sob stories, wanting him to be the loving little brother she longed for. Too bad. Women were easy targets with their need to be loved, and he'd made it a long way in life taking advantage of their weakness.

Finished, he examined his handiwork. A dark look twisted his face. He showed mercy with Neely's Café, but there would be no mercy this time.

FORTY-SEVEN

FBI agent Mark Ryerson knocked on the sheriff's office door. Looking up, Dan nodded for him to enter.

Showing his ID, the man introduced himself. "Mark Ryerson, FBI, St. Louis branch. I'm here to investigate, and perhaps facilitate an arrest in the murder of Macon Baytree. We were called in due to conflict-of-interest regarding the main suspect."

Dan looked at the gray-suited man across the desk. Slightly built with thinning red hair combed straight back from a high forehead, the agent's brown eyes were steady, and the sheriff noted the cool, almost arrogant, appraisal as they studied him. Irritation prickled his scalp.

"Conflict-of-interest? We're still trying to decipher the security video, trying to sort out and identify who was in the room and who left. Hopefully your tip explained the room was near dark, curtain was closed, and someone had sprayed adhesive bandage spray on the lens. We have very poor feed results. What does the FBI have that we don't?"

Agent Ryerson spoke bluntly. "In fact, we have received a tip that your wife is the most likely suspect in this murder. I'm here to question her and investigate, see if there's enough evidence to make the arrest."

Dan shook his head. Bile rose, burning his throat. Looking at the agent with disgust, he managed to keep his voice calm.

"A tip saying my wife committed the murder? Are you crazy? She was almost nine months pregnant. I suspect she would have stood out even in the blurred video if we'd seen her, which we did not." Scowling, he stared at the agent.

"It's still necessary to interview her, sir. If you like, we can do it here, or at your home." He wasn't asking.

Furious, Dan stood. "Follow me," he growled, clapping his Stetson on his head and storming out of his office.

"Headed home, Vicki," he said. "Randy's in charge until I get back. No calls."

The two men headed out the door, Dan talking on his cell phone as he walked across the parking lot.

Hilldale Farewell

Molly waited by the screen door and watched as the two vehicles pulled into the driveway. Her green eyes held the stormy look of fear, and as Dan climbed the steps his heart ached for his wife, for their child, for himself.

He knew she was innocent, but how could he prove it when he knew she had been at the hospital with her grandfather? He didn't know exactly where Molly had been—and the security video was dark and blurred enough that a few of the fast-moving responders to Macon's room were unidentifiable.

The agent could try to say that one of them was Molly, and she could be arrested. Taking his wife in his arms, he whispered, "It'll be all right, love. Just answer his questions so he can be on his way."

The three entered the small living room and Molly offered the men sweet tea.

"I only drink un-sweetened tea, ma'am," Agent Ryerson said, his face a closed mask.

"I have some made. Most folks I've met from St. Louis like it un-sweetened, so I made a batch, just in case…" her voice trembled and she didn't finish, but turned and headed for the kitchen. She returned with their tea and a plate of sliced zucchini bread.

Ryerson took a slice, bit into it and picked up his glass of tea. "Mrs. Halloran, I need to ask you a few questions regarding your whereabouts at the time of Macon Baytree's death. Were you at the hospital?" Chewing, he studied her face, noted the paleness highlighting her freckles.

"I was. My grandfather was dying, and I spent the day—I spent days with him."

"Did you leave his room on the day of Macon Baytree's murder? Can anyone verify that you were with your grandfather and didn't leave the floor to pay a visit to Mr. Baytree? After all, he is the one suspected of beating Mr. Sumday, resulting in his death." His voice held a note of accusation and Molly's mouth went dry.

"I went to the nurses' station to read his chart. The head nurse, Ruth Hanson saw me, we talked. Then I went to the restroom and headed back to Grampa's room. There was a guard there. I can't remember his name, but I'm sure you can check it out."

"How long did it take you to leave the nurses' station, use the restroom, and arrive back in your grandfather's room?" Ryerson reached for another slice of bread and Dan was tempted to slap it out of his hand.

"I—I don't know," Molly closed her eyes. "I didn't check the clock, didn't think about how long it took me. Besides," she looked at the agent, "I didn't even know that awful man was in the hospital until I got back to Grampa's room and the guard told me."

Agent Ryerson wiped his fingers on a napkin from the tray, drank the rest of his tea, and stood. "We understand the murder was committed by someone who is familiar with medical procedures, shooting enough air into a main vein to kill him. I've read that's not an easy thing to do—I mean, knowing how much air to use to cause an embolism."

He studied her face. "You have that expertise, and even in your condition, could have made it to his room and back before anyone noticed. You had motive, as well."

Nodding to her, he turned to Dan. "Sheriff, I'll look at the security video you have now, and Mrs. Halloran, please don't leave town. I may be back." The hint of arrest lay dark and cold between them.

Dan stood and nodded the agent toward the door. With Ryerson waiting on the porch, Dan took Molly in his arms. "He's got nothing and he knows it. I'll be back this afternoon. Call me if you need me. Lock up after me. I love you."

Molly followed the men with her eyes, watching them leave, the feeling of guilt enveloping her. She hadn't killed Macon Baytree, but she'd wanted him dead. And now she was being accused of his murder.

Just then, Billy let out a whimper, gearing up for a good cry if his diaper and hunger weren't taken care of soon. Grateful to have something else to think about, she headed to the bedroom to rescue her son.

FORTY-EIGHT

Roxanne Blythe sat in the interrogation room, a suffocating cloud of silence surrounding her. She pulled at a hangnail. Straightened her uniform. Pushed the bobby pins more securely into her gray-streaked bun resting at the nape of her neck. She took deep breaths to try and calm her nerves.

The sheriff's deputy had met her at the hospital parking lot and requested she come to the office in Hilldale for questioning. She knew why. Even with a stolen name tag and blurring the security camera, they'd figured out she was the nurse who'd drugged the guard and helped James escape.

It was foolish for her to think she'd get away with it. She always paid a price for helping Jimmy clean up his messes. A deep sadness filled her. They'd learned her connection to her step-brother, and he wasn't going to help her. And he wasn't going to give up his war on Hilldale.

She'd known him most of his life, tried to love him enough to change him, but he couldn't give up his cruelty and hatred, his need to have revenge, to control everything and everyone around him.

And, she had helped him escape.

She had thought of making a run for it, trying to get to her car and go where? Too late for that. Instead, she had nodded to the nice young man and told him she would meet him at the sheriff's office.

"I'm sorry, ma'am, but I've been instructed to bring you in myself. We'll bring you back to your vehicle after your interview." Randy Carter had led the way to his SUV.

Following, Roxanne knew she'd never get back to her car. Helping her step-brother escape had been stupid, but then, she had always tried to help him.

Shaking her head, she realized, once again he'd used her, and left her to clean up his mess. She knew there would be no cleaning up this one.

FORTY-NINE

Manuel listened to his daughter explain why she'd decided to return to the Taylor ranch in Texas. He listened as she begged him to come along, his heart aching, for her loss, and his.

He knew his job would be easily filled; the apartment would rent quickly. But he knew he couldn't go back to Texas, or to the Taylor ranch. Not ever again.

Carmen searched her father's face. Seeing the sadness in his eyes, she reached for his hand.

"Papa, I can't stay here. Justin will bring me back for the trial, but I can't do my job, can't work in that courthouse again, can't..." she stopped. "I'm sorry. I sound like a wimp. You raised me better than this, but—but I think I'm broken." Tears overflowed and she used her shirt-sleeve to wipe them away.

"Never mind, *mi querida hija*. Do what you must to get through this, to heal." He squeezed her hand.

"*Your loving daughter*," she repeated. "I don't feel so loving, Papa, leaving you. I feel like I'm running away. Maybe I am.

"I've overstayed my welcome here at the farm. They've been so kind to let me stay while the sheriff goes after that man. It's horrible how he escaped. But, I must to go, Papa. I have to.

"Justin said I'll be safe at the ranch. Baytree won't find me in Texas. I can move back to the casita I grew up in, no strings attached. Come with us, Papa? Please?"

Manuel sighed. "I wish I could. You must do what you need to. I will be fine. Let me help you get packed. These are fine people, but I will be happy for you to go with Justin back home. Perhaps, one day I will join you there. Right now, my job is here." His lies cut through him, shaming him, breaking his heart.

Standing, he helped Carmen to her feet and the two embraced. Manuel knew this was *despedida*--farewell, for he would never see his daughter again. He fought to keep his tears in check until he was on the gravel road headed back to Hilldale.

Pat Jaeger

FIFTY

Pastor Hughes finished his message and called for those who wanted prayer to come forward. The choir sang softly as parishioners filed up the aisle to kneel at the altar. Elders and deacons joined the pastor, laying hands on the bowed heads, quietly praying for each one.

Dan rose and helped Molly outside, his arm around her shoulder. Billy slept soundly through the service, snuggled against his mother, but now began to fuss as the trio headed to their pick-up.

Folks trickled from the church doors, and Dan could hear the music pick up volume as the prayers ended and the rest of the congregation began to disperse. He settled Molly, then strapped Billy into his car seat, flashing back to the young couple he'd watched years ago, leaving the hospital when Muley had been shot. At the time, he'd wondered if he'd ever have a family of his own.

Smiling, he realized how blessed he was. He had everything he'd dreamed of, and then some. Walking to the driver's side, he looked up as Carter and Tina Neely called out and waved. Waving back, he pulled his door open.

A sudden and terrible rumble shook the ground. Dan looked up to see the rear of the church fly skyward, stained glass shards glittering in the beautiful morning sun. An earsplitting thunder followed with a roar of flame, and then screams. He began to run.

Carter sat on the ground, Tina in his arms. Blood trickled from a wound in her back where a piece of wood imbedded deep into her body. Even as he knelt beside them, her eyes, staring at her life-long love, clouded over and Carter cried out. Dan kept moving.

People—his people, lay littered across the churchyard, broken and bleeding, weeping and screaming. Children cried out for their parents, some who lay on top of them protecting them from the flying debris. The carnage was horrific.

Calling his department for help, he did what he could to tend to the wounded, still trying to work his way into the wreckage of what was once their place of worship.

He knew tears washed down his face, but he couldn't stop them, couldn't dry them. He had to get inside. Muley, Mary and Wanda Harmon, Gordie and his family had lingered behind with the choir, and Dan had to find them. Had to save them.

Entering the gaping hole where once the doors had been, he found Muley laying across Miss Mary and Wanda Harmon. Gently lifting him, he saw the two women were shaken, maybe bruised, but otherwise, appeared to be okay. Muley lay unconscious in his arms, a large swelling turning dark blue, blossomed on the back of his head.

Wanda Harmon struggled to sit up. "Give 'em to me," she said, her voice rough with emotion. "Go find the children. Go on, now," she ordered. Dan shifted Muley until he lay in her arms, cradled in her lap. Mary moved up next to her sister-in-law.

"Don't wait too long," Dan told her. That fire's creeping this way. Thank the Lord it's not the inferno it started out to be. Still, don't wait..." he looked down at Muley.

"We're fine, Dan. Go on. We'll look after Muley until help gets here. Drag 'em out, if we have to!"

Nodding, Dan rose and looked down the aisle toward where the altar should have been. Bodies lay sprawled and shattered, many partially buried beneath wood, and brick, and shingles, the overhead sprinklers adding to the chaotic mess.

Moans, cries for help, screams of pain echoed. Looking around, he began to lift a splintered beam. Freeing the people beneath it, he found them unresponsive.

Step-by-step, he made his way through the rubble lit by sunlight from the missing back wall and gaping hole in the roof, praying the sprinklers left working, would keep the fire from spreading until they could get everyone out of the building.

"Here!" he heard someone call. Looking toward where the choir had been, he saw Gordie standing, blood running from several wounds. "Here, help me, Sheriff Dan."

The two worked to lift broken beams and bricks from their neighbors. As they worked, Dan heard sirens. Help had arrived and he focused on finding survivors in the rubble. Heart aching, he prayed he'd find Juanita and Little Wanda before Gordie did.

Rescuers began to remove the wounded and take them to a triage tent set up in the parking lot. Those who no longer needed help were left, a blanket covering their remains. Dan saw Muley carried out, Mary and Wanda close behind. He heard Gordie choke out the names of his wife and daughter. No one answered above the cries of the wounded and dying.

Dan made his way to where the upright piano lay belly down. Catching a glimpse of bright red curls, his heart lurched and caught. Scrambling over a pile of debris, he squatted down to look beneath where the keyboard met the floor, creating a tiny cave-like space. Inside, eyes wide, Little Wanda stared out.

"Ma's trapped, Uncle Danny. I can't get her out. She's sleeping."

"Okay, love," he said, "I'll lift this and you scoot out and go to your pa. He's right behind me. Go straight to him, Little Wanda, hear me?"

Nodding, she answered, "Will my mama be okay? I tried to do the healing song for her, but she still won't wake up."

"Never mind, sweetheart. I'll get your mama out of there. You mind what I said. Soon as I lift this up, you scoot out and find your pa. You can walk, can't you?" He hoped she was as uninjured as she sounded.

"Yep, I can, Uncle Danny. I'm ready."

Dan grasped the front of the piano and lifted, straining to hold the heavy instrument while Little Wanda crawled from beneath it.

"Go to your pa, child," he grunted, exertion setting the muscles in his shoulders and arms on fire, bringing beads of sweat to his face.

Little Wanda, wobbly but able to walk, moved across the debris and called to her father. Gordie looked up from where he was helping the pastor from beneath the overturned pulpit. Agony and joy lit his face as he watched his daughter moving toward him. Spying Dan, he realized the sheriff was trying to hold the piano up, but was losing his grip.

Gordie settled the pastor against the pulpit and grabbed his daughter, hugging her until she squealed for her pa to put her down.

"Run outside and find help for the pastor, Little Wanda," he said. "Sing for folks outside, but don't come back in here. That fire is moving this way. Run, Little Wanda." And then he headed toward the sheriff.

Gripping the other end of the piano, the two men hoisted it up and tilted it away from the crumpled figure beneath it. Gasping for air, heart-wrenching sounds of agony pouring from him, Gordie dropped to his knees and touched the lifeless face beneath the bright red curls. Cold and still, eyes closed, his beloved wife lay before him.

Sobs racked his body as he carefully wormed his arm beneath her, lifting her to his chest. Holding her against him, he begged Dan to get a paramedic, someone to help Juanita.

Turning, Dan saw two paramedics entering the front, their stretcher in tow. "Here," he shouted at them. "Help us here."

Kneeling next to Gordie, he gently moved Juanita's body away from him enough to check the pulse in her neck. Nothing. Fear exploded in his head—his chest, shooting through his body, but he forced himself to remain calm. "Let her down, Gordie. Let me try to revive her. Let her down," he ordered.

Gordie obeyed, and as the paramedics reached them, Dan moved aside. "I can't find a pulse," was all he could manage.

"Sheriff, help us lay her flat."

Dan nodded. Looking at the medic he was surprised to see it was Andrea, the medic who had years before, helped them rescue a young girl from the secret room of a depraved kidnapper. She nodded to him, then focused on the woman lying before her.

The two medics began to work on the still form. Gordie, weeping, refused to leave her and go to his daughter, motioning for his friend to go. Dan understood. He saw the child hadn't left. Moving over the debris, he watched as she held the hand of the pastor, quietly singing her healing song. Color had bloomed in the wounded man's face, and his eyes fluttered.

"Look, Uncle Danny, he's waking up." Smiling up at him, her eyes clouded. "Mama?"

"I don't know, sweetheart. The paramedics are with her and your pa. They'll do the best they can for your ma."

Little Wanda closed her eyes, said a quick prayer, appeared to listen for a moment, then looked at the sheriff. "She's going to be okay. God told me what to do, what to say. And I sang to her, Uncle Danny. She'll be okay."

Dan nodded and reminded her she was to leave the building and run to the safety of the triage tent. With a heavy heart, he returned to where Gordie wept, the small group clustered around Juanita, trying to revive her.

"One more time," Andy said, her hands placing the paddles on Juanita's chest. "Clear!"

The machine snapped electricity into the still woman, causing her body to buck. The medics watched the machine, looking for signs of a heartbeat to start up. Nothing.

A small voice interrupted them. Pushing her way through, Little Wanda knelt next to her mother and laid her hand on her heart. The medics started to move her away, but halted. Something about the stillness, the focus of the child before them silenced their objections.

Her voice quiet, but clear, Little Wanda spoke. "Ma, you got to wake up now. It's time. You got to wake up and come home with Pa and me. God told me you can wake up, so wake up now." Tears rolled down her face, but she seemed not to notice as she sat before the body of her mother.

Andy moved to hold the child. Gordie moved to take his daughter in his arms. Dan moved to lift her up and carry her away from the tragic scene. But Little Wanda sat still, her hand on her mother, her tiny voice singing softly.

A shudder rolled through Juanita's body. She coughed. Moaned. Opened her eyes. Golden eyes met golden eyes.

"You called me," she said, her voice tired, weak. "I was so far away, I wasn't sure I could get back to you, but I heard you call me, and I came."

Little Wanda lay her head on her mother's breast and felt her mother's fingers bury themselves in her tangled curls. "Mama," was all she said.

The paramedics and Dan stared in wonder at the scene before them. Then, a cry from the pastor called them to where he'd found a choir member still alive in the rubble. Hurrying away, Dan stopped long enough to stare at the miracle amidst the devastation.

FIFTY-ONE

James Baytree lay still. Moving brought on terrible agony in his chest. His bomb worked well—too well. He laughed mirthlessly. A wooden splinter the size of his hand had imbedded itself in his chest. He hadn't gotten far enough away. He'd wanted to watch the devastation he'd wrought, and now he was a victim of his own bomb. He coughed and blood spurted from his mouth.

He heard shouting and rough hands turned him over. Someone yelled for help and then the sheriff stood over him, calling him by name. Baytree closed his eyes. *End of the road.*

Pain crashed like violent waves as he was lifted and laid on a stretcher. Loaded into an ambulance, he could hear the medics talking, reading his vitals.

Die! he ordered himself. Instead, his heart kept beating, his uninjured lung kept bringing him oxygen. *Die*! he ordered again. This time there was no conviction in the order, and James Baytree felt the darkness roll over him.

FIFTY-TWO

Carmen sat on the edge of her bed. Packed and waiting for Gordie and family to come home from church before Justin picked her up, she looked around her room, out the large window near her bed. Sunshine lit the oak and sycamore trees, poured in her window warming the cold that had engulfed her, holding her captive since her abduction.

She would miss the child. Little Wanda had brought her back to the land of the living, though she'd come reluctantly, painfully. The hurting wasn't over, Carmen knew that, but she knew she was healing. Could feel it in her body, in her mind, in her heart. There was a stirring in her bones, a new song beginning within her that she couldn't quite sing yet.

Damaged, yes. Broken, yes. But not beyond repair. She acknowledged to herself, she would never be the same woman again, but she would continue healing, continue facing the challenges of rising every day and looking in the mirror at the scarred face and haunted eyes that now belonged to her. And she would learn to love herself again.

Little Wanda and her family had brought her laughter. Had made her feel despite her desire to keep her heart hardened against more hurt. When the child had placed her small hands on Carmen's face, had looked into her eyes with love and joy, she'd felt that stirring inside her, a bit of melting of the icy fear and the cold dread of rising each day to remember. The gentle touch, the unconditional love as Little Wanda had traced her tiny finger over her damaged face—this, in spite of the painfulness of it, made her long to live again.

It was difficult. Sometimes agonizingly so. Yet, somehow, she knew she would be all right. Maybe, like the little girl repeated many times over the weeks, God really did care about her, really would bless her with healing inside and out. Somehow, she believed she would get beyond what had happened to her, and not just survive, but she would reclaim her life. Sighing, she picked at a piece of lint that clung to her jeans.

Justin. He was late getting back from church. Looking out the window at the beauty and peace that surrounded her, she thought of the man she had loved since she was a child. Justin. He made her long to love again—like a woman, like a wife. Shivering in the warm morning sun, she closed her eyes.

It terrified her to go beyond the thinking. She still trembled or flinched at every touch. Still woke up soaked in fear, chest hurting with labored breathing, heart pounding, mind panicked. But she longed to feel that love again, and that was a start.

The sun traveled across the braided rug and lay warm on her as she waited. Downstairs, the screen door slammed and heavy footsteps climbed the stairs. Carmen stood, ready to take the next step.

FIFTY-THREE

James Baytree woke up in a dimly lit room. *Hospital.* Groaning, he tried, but failed, to turn on his side, restricted by heavy bandaging, pain, and shackles binding him to the railings of the bed. A guard sat next to the bed staring at him.

"I got to use the toilet," he croaked, his throat dry and scratchy.

"You got a catheter. Anything else, you use the bed pan." The guard's voice hung in the air between them, like a challenge. "Act like an animal, get treated like an animal," he growled.

James tried to work up enough spit to spew at the guard, but his mouth was too dry. "Gimme a drink," he ordered, his face contorted with fury.

The guard stood, retrieved a cup of water with a straw in it, held it to Baytree's lips, and waited for him to drink his fill.

Laying back on his pillow, the prisoner looked around. He hoped Roxy was on duty and he could convince her to help him again. She'd be disappointed he hadn't left, but he usually got around her objections with a little smooth talking.

The door swooshed open and Sheriff Dan Halloran strode into the room. Baytree frowned and turned his face toward the wall. "Get out of my room," he growled, still not looking at the sheriff. "I'm too sick to talk to you. Get out!"

"Yeah, I can see how sick you are," Dan said, nodding to the guard, sending him out for a coffee break. "Almost blew yourself up with the rest of the folks you murdered." His words delivered cold and hard, his eyes steady on the man laying before him. Try as he might, Dan felt no compassion for Baytree, his injuries, the life he would serve in prison, the fact he had no family but his step-sister to mourn for him.

Removing his Stetson, he sat next to the bed, hat in hand. Clearing his throat, he looked at Baytree and wondered what had turned this man into such a monster.

He'd destroyed the lives of so many people, including, Dan believed, his deceased wives, yet he appeared to have no remorse. He'd led his son down the same path, encouraging hate and murder. What kind of father instilled such things in his son? He cleared his throat again.

"Says somewhere in Proverbs that when you lay a trap for others, you're going to get caught in it yourself. Your hurtful ways are coming home to roost.

"James Baytree, you're under arrest for multiple murders, bombings, assault-with-intent—shoot—there's too many charges for me to remember. We'll have it in writing for you and your lawyer." He read him his rights and sat back in the chair, lightly tapping the brim of his hat.

"If you're waiting for your step-sister, Roxanne, you're going to be disappointed. She's sitting in jail, thanks to you. Looking at accessory to murder and such. She trusted you to leave and not hurt anyone else—her words. Reckon you taught her a lesson she'll live with the rest of her life."

Baytree scowled when he heard the news about Roxy. *Stupid woman to get herself caught.* "Don't worry, I got other help, Sheriff. I ain't gonna never stand trial, and once I'm gone, you ain't never gonna see me again. I done paid your pitiful town back for messing with me and taking my horses, and for killing my boy. I get shet of this place, I'm gone."

The sneer on his face told Dan that this man had no remorse for the lives he'd destroyed, he just felt sorry for himself. How could one man bring about so much evil affecting so many people? Shaking his head, he stood and looked down on the man he'd wanted dead. And if he dared think the truth, still wanted dead. The man he nearly killed, if it hadn't been for Justin Taylor stepping in.

Sadness swept the hatred away. What a terrible life it must be to spend it filled with so much rage and hate, not knowing how to love, or be loved. Now he'd have terrible consequences for the choices he'd made. Dan shrugged. He couldn't fix this man, nor did he have the desire to do so, but still, sorrow for Baytree's lostness gentled his next words.

"Guards are posted outside the door, along the hallway, and in your room. Give it a try, if you want, but I guarantee you, you're not escaping again." Dan waited as the guard entered, steaming cup of coffee in hand, then turned and walked out of the room, tugging his Stetson low over his eyes.

At the end of the hallway, he noticed Manuel Fuentes mopping the tile floor. Surprised, he nodded.

"Mr. Fuentes! I thought you worked for the courthouse. I hear your daughter is leaving for Texas. Good to know she's doing better."

Manuel looked up at the sheriff and nodded. "Sí," he said, "She was going to leave Sunday, but the bombing—" he shrugged. "It is terrible what that man has done to so many people. It is terrible what he has done to my Carmen. He is an evil man, Sheriff."

"Reckon you're right," Dan replied. "He'll spend the rest of his life in prison for what he's done." Touching the brim of his hat, he pushed through the stairway door and left the hospital, something nagging at the back of his mind.

FIFTY-FOUR

Juanita looked at her husband and smiled. "Stop fussing, Gordie. I'm fine. No broken bones, a few bruises. I don't need to be in the hospital to rest, I need to be home with you, with Little Wanda."

At the mention of her daughter, her voice caught. "What do you think happened?" Her eyes darkened. "I was so far away, and this beautiful light glowed up ahead. I heard Little Wanda calling me, but I was so tired, Gordie." She looked up at her husband.

"I saw this man-like being, full of light. Every strand of hair, every bit of him exuded light. He told me it wasn't time for me to come with Him, I needed to go back." Her voice caught. Her eyes locked on Gordie's, "I didn't want to—I didn't want to come back."

Juanita reached for Gordie's hand. He knelt and wrapped his arms around her, waiting.

"That was at first, you know, that I didn't want to come back. Then Little Wanda's voice got louder and I knew I had to come back home where I was loved, was needed. But, this place, Gordie, it was so beautiful." Her voice broke and she laid her head on his shoulder. "I'm sorry."

"It's okay, I know what you mean. Sometimes when I have one of my *angel taps*, I wake up reluctant to be here in this world. But, we have a daughter to raise, and what a girl!" He laughed into Juanita's curls, inhaling the smell of her shampoo.

"She's a special one, she is. God give her to us, and I knew it the first time He showed me I was to be part of you all's lives. We got to look out for her, protect her, 'cause most folks ain't going to understand her gift." He held his wife tight, silent in their love for one another, and for their child.

FIFTY-FIVE

James Baytree watched the television overhead, his mind trying to work out a plan of escape. Too many guards. Roxy locked up. Might have to make a break for it during court, or from the jail house, once he was healed enough to be transferred.

His door opened and the guard turned to see who entered. "Housekeeping," said the man in uniform, pushing a bucket of water with a mop immersed in strong-smelling fluid that quickly engulfed the room. The guard grunted.

"Geez, that smell!" He checked the man's ID. "Looks good. I'll leave you to it. This guy ain't going nowhere, but stay back from him, he's tricky.

"I'm going to send one of the guys from down the hallway in here. I gotta go see a man about a horse, if you know what I mean."

He quickly left and headed for the restroom, leaving Manuel Fuentes alone with the man who'd violated his precious daughter.

This time, Fuentes didn't bother to blur the cameras. He knew he only had seconds to complete this final mission, and he wanted the cameras to record that he, Manuel Fuentes, had avenged his daughter.

Swiftly, before the new guard arrived, he lifted a huge syringe from the cleaning water, pulled the plunger back, drawing in a tube full of air. One step brought him to James Baytree's side. Looking in the man's face just registering knowledge of what was happening, Manuel locked eyes with him.

"This is for my daughter, Carmen Fuentes. You will die for what you have done." Baytree had no time to cry for help. One hand pressed hard against the prisoner's nose and mouth, the other plunged the needle and injected air into the struggling man's juggler vein. Manual quickly removed it, tossing the syringe back into the water.

Watching as Baytree's body thrashed, then shuddered, then quieted, Fuentes prayed the man was truly, finally dead. He heard footsteps approaching and swiped his drenched mop a few times, thoroughly wetting the tiles. As the door opened, he pushed his pail towards the guard blocking his view of the prisoner.

"Excuse me, señor." Looking over his shoulder, he said, "He is asleep. The floor is *muy mojado*—very wet. Be careful."

The guard let Manuel through the door. "Whew! That stuff stinks something awful. I'll just wait out here a few minutes until the floor dries and that smell dissipates," he said, settling in the chair next to the door.

Manuel moved quickly down the hallway to the janitor's closet. Leaving the mop and bucket inside, he pulled his uniform shirt off, slid on a doctor's white jacket and draped a stethoscope around his neck. Stepping back into the hallway, he made his way down the stairs, exiting the hospital.

Bags packed and waiting on the rear truck seat, bank account emptied with the cash stashed in his glove compartment, Manuel Fuentes began the long drive south, all the way to Mexico.

FIFTY-SIX

Carmen's hands flew to her mouth, stifling a cry. "Baytree? He bombed the church?"

Justin took her into his arms and held her trembling body close as she tried to digest the horrific news.

"That's why I'm so late. Helped as much as I could until the troops got there. Boone and Cole Counties sent everyone they could spare. It's going to take a while to recover everyone. At least fourteen have been found so far. The bomb and fire destroyed the building and everything in it."

Whispering, Carmen asked, "Little Wanda? Her parents?"

"Okay. They're getting checked out to be sure there's no serious injuries, but I think they'll be back here this evening. Mind if we stay another day or two, see if there's anything we can help them with?"

Mumbling her assent into his shoulder, Justin felt her trembling ease. Grateful, he turned her enough to look in her eyes.

"Got Baytree in the hospital under guard. No way to escape this time. It'll soon be over, Carmen, and you won't have to give that man a second thought."

Carmen sat down. Her heart pounded in her ears and she felt light-headed.

Justin watched her twist her hands in her lap. Looking at him, her face pale, eyes haunted, she swallowed hard.

"Coming back to testify is going to be difficult, but I will do it, and be glad when he's locked up for good. With this bombing, so many injured, so many dead—that's mass murder. He could get the death penalty."

"It's a good possibility," Justin agreed. "Now, let's go get some supper in Jefferson City. You need some protein. I found this great barbeque place, and I know how you love your barbequed ribs. Besides, I want to arrange for the owner to cater a couple of meals to city hall where all the ER crews are gathering. We'll bring back some extras for Gordie and the family."

He took her hand and helped her stand. The two moved down the stairs, side-by-side, Justin's arm holding his love steady.

FIFTY-SEVEN

Agent Mark Ryerson stood on the porch waiting for one of the Hallorans to open the door. An autopsy would verify what the hospital security footage had shown him. Carmen Fuentes' father had murdered James Baytree, and it appeared he had also murdered the son, Macon. The method of death for both was identical, and the syringe had been found in the filthy mop water.

The door opened. Sheriff Dan Halloran stared out the screen at him making no attempt to invite him in.

"What can I do for you, Agent?" he asked, his voice weary, his face lined with grief.

"Courtesy call," Ryerson replied. "Manuel Fuentes is shown on the security footage killing Baytree. He didn't try to hide his face this time. Since it's the identical method used on the son, we are seeking his arrest for both murders. Just letting you know, your wife is no longer a suspect."

He cleared his throat. "Sorry if I came across a bit harsh before. It's my job to catch criminals, not make friends." With that, he nodded, turned on his heel and headed for his vehicle. Dan watched until the gray Ford backed out of the driveway and headed out of town.

When the office had called with the news of Baytree's death, Dan had felt a surge of emotions tumbling over each other. He'd gone to the hospital, reviewed the security video, identifying Carmen's father as the man in the hospital room.

He should have known. Chastising himself, remembering passing Fuentes in the hallway, he'd had the gut-feeling he was missing something.

The manhunt was on. His department was cooperating with the FBI, and U. S. Marshall Justin Taylor would be bringing Carmen in for interviews, but Dan doubted her father would be caught any time soon.

Fuentes had a good head-start, his abandoned truck found in a ditch, leading authorities to believe he had changed vehicles somewhere south of Joplin. No further sightings had been reported.

He felt sad for Fuentes taking the law into his hands, committing murder. Still, he couldn't help hoping he made it across the Mexican border—for

Carmen's sake, as well as her father's. Dan wasn't a fan of vigilante justice, but he couldn't judge what he himself would be capable of, if someone did to Molly and Billy what Baytree had done to Fuentes' daughter.

He realized, just from the attack on Molly, that he himself could have taken Baytree's life, if Justin Taylor hadn't stopped him. He prayed he would never be in that position again. And, he prayed for Manuel Fuentes, that God's justice be done. Shaking loose of the sadness, he looked at his wife and son thanking God for their lives, for allowing him to have them in his life.

Molly sat on the couch, legs tucked up beneath her, her hair pulled up into a long, dark pony tail. To him, she looked like a young girl, vulnerable, and his breath caught with the surge of love he felt for her.

Billy lay across her lap gazing into her face. Dan watched as his wife gently traced their son's cheeks, tiny pug nose, perfect ears. The baby smiled. Looking up at Dan, she grinned, her face lit with wonder.

"Did you see that? His first real smile. You can't attribute that one to gas! What a smart, sweet boy you are," she cooed to the baby. Dan laughed. Amidst all the sorrow and devastation surrounding them, God sent golden beams of joy to touch them; to renew their hope, as He lifted them from the ashes of destruction.

Horror of the worst kind had invaded Hilldale, threatening to destroy the small town with death and terror, leaving hate and revenge in its wake.

Determination tightened Dan's jaw. Prayers filled his heart and mind. He looked at his wife's face, at his son lying happy in his mother's lap, gurgling and cooing, the sounds at once wrenching and soothing his heart. He knew he was blessed, and he was grateful.

A strange mixture of sorrow and joy washed through him, and for just a moment, he was swept with fear and love for his family, his town.

Taking the baby's feet into his hands, he gently massaged the tiny toes, feeling the wonder and the blessing of the gift of Billy's life.

There would be much suffering and pain, much to mend and rebuild, but looking at his wife and son, Dan knew, with God's guidance and strength, he would help his town get through the horror of the past few months, and rise from the ashes of their lives to feel joy and peace.

FIFTY-EIGHT

Justin and Carmen stood close, his arm firm around her, she, leaning into him. In front of them, Dan, his deputy, Randy Carter, and Roxanne Blythe, handcuffed, stood silent in the warm morning sun. A cloud passed overhead and Roxanne shivered.

The tiny group watched as a small skid loader began to fill the grave before them. The thud of the clods hitting the coffin below had the sound of finality. Carmen Fuentes drew in a deep breath, slowly blowing it out.

Over. A solitary tear rolled down her gaunt cheek, following the path of a still-raw scar left by the boot of the man in the grave. The cloud drifted past and the sun caught the teardrop, sending tiny shafts of sunlight out into the day. *Over*, she repeated to herself.

*****

"Over," Roxanne whispered. Sighing, she watched the remains of the only family she had left disappear under the clumps of Missouri clay. She'd asked the sheriff if she could attend James's burial—there would be no funeral. He'd agreed, and Roxanne felt grateful when he'd arrived to take her to the tiny county cemetery where their parents and Macon were buried.

"I thought you might want to place these on your step-brother's grave," Sheriff Halloran had said, showing her a lovely mixed fall bouquet tied together with a ribbon that had LOVE written on it. She'd cried then, trying to thank him, her words failing.

And now here she was, burying the last of her kin, and headed for many years in prison.

She felt the handcuffs snap loose, and the sheriff handed her the bouquet. Nodding toward the grave, now full, he allowed her to walk alone to the mound of dirt where she placed the flowers at James Baytree's grave head. "Over," she said to him. "It's over."

*****

Dan watched Roxanne lay the flowers lovingly on her step-brother's grave. The smell of the freshly-turned soil filled the morning air and smelled like the promise of new life. He felt sadness for the woman in front of him, but he could not feel anything but grateful the man who'd tormented Hilldale was gone.

He'd found a note in Baytree's pocket, no doubt meant to be found somewhere near the bombing scene. It read: **Farewell Hilldale**. Dan believed Baytree meant it as a death threat to the town and its folks. He reached into his pocket and withdrew a note he'd written to Baytree.

Randy re-cuffed Roxanne, as Dan stepped forward. Placing the note on the damp soil, he took a large clod and placed it on the paper to keep it from blowing away.

*****

As the small group left the cemetery, U. S. Marshall Justin Taylor caught a glimpse of the words

149

printed in bold black ink: **FAREWELL, JAMES BAYTREE. GOD FORGIVE YOU.**

Shaking his head, he led his love away from the grave and into the new day. God would have to help him forgive Baytree; he was unable to—yet. For now, it was enough for him to let the hate and fury go, to let the breath of Life sweep through him.

Carmen's hand, cold and damp with the morning's emotions, slipped into his. He looked down into her dark brown eyes, rejoicing at the look she returned. His heart filled with gratitude, and as they walked to their vehicles, he never looked back.

FIFTY-NINE

"Ma, did you see Jesus?" Little Wanda sat cuddled in her mother's lap, the two setting the old rocker into motion.

Juanita held her daughter against her. She nestled her chin in the wild red curls that encircled the child's head.

"I'm not sure who it was I saw. Never thought about what He would look like, but the being I saw when I—when—I—" Juanita couldn't bring herself to say the word.

"When you died—like Grampa Billy? Like Miss Tina?" Little Wanda finished for her. "It's okay, I know about dying, Mama. It's part of the healing song. Some folks don't think dying is healing, but I do 'cause I know where I'm going." She looked up at her mother. "So do you." Little Wanda smiled.

"God told me to call you back, that He wasn't ready for you. He said, 'Little Wanda, you call your mother loud and sure, no doubt in your heart, and she will hear you and come home.' So I did it!"

She sighed and snuggled against Juanita's breast. "He knows my name, Ma. God knows my name."

Rocking gently, the two sat quiet, their hearts and minds on the miracle granted to them. Juanita struggled with the fact of her heart stopping, of walking toward the beautiful light, of meeting the light-filled being. Jesus? She didn't know, but suspected it was so.

Why her? That horrible day so many died. Three children, Mark Calvin, the teen boy who sang in the choir despite being teased by the other teens. Adults, friends, neighbors, folks she'd come to know and love from working in Neely's Café. And, Tina. Juanita felt the tears start.

Why her? Why did God spare her? she asked herself again. She was a nobody, not important except maybe to Gordie and Little Wanda, her Gramma Wanda, and Aunt Mary. Little Wanda shifted and snuggled deeper into her lap. Her daughter. A child who listened and obeyed God's voice.

Juanita trembled at the magnitude of what that meant. She feared for this tiny little girl who brought love and healing to everyone she could. Pushing the rocker back into motion, she closed her eyes. Listening to the gentle snores of the child in her lap, Juanita prayed.

SIXTY

Muley sat with Oscar Sumday, wondering how to tell Billy's boy what happened all them long years ago. He swiped his hand across his bald pate wincing when he hit the still-tender bruise and swelling. *Blessed to be alive.*

Once his friend told him about the accident, he and Billy Sumday had never talked again about the day his wife died. Now his old friend and adopted brother had charged him with telling Oscar the truth. Asked on his death bed! Muley groaned. Oscar looked at him.

"You okay, Mr. Burger?"

"Reckon you could call me Uncle Muley, or plain ol' Muley, eh?" Muley looked at the man across from him. Picking up his iced tea, he swallowed some, stalling.

"What is it my father wanted you to tell me, Mr. umm, Uncle Muley? I've packed the cabin up, distributed the things he wanted me to, and put the cabin and the acreage in William Daniel Halloran's name." He shook his head. "He knew about the baby, even the name, long before Molly became pregnant. His will is dated three years ago."

Muley chuckled. "Oh, your pa knew things, all right. Used to vex me something fierce when he'd do stuff like that. But he never used his knowing for meanness." Looking at the man across from him, he sighed again.

"Your pa charged me with telling you about the day your ma died. Charged me on his death bed, he did. Didn't want to do it. Still don't want to do it. Never talked about it after it happened—not ever."

Oscar sat up straighter in his chair. He reached for his glass of tea, his hand trembling. "I don't remember much about that day even though the police report and newspaper articles say I was there. I saw a picture of me when they found us. I looked so scared, so lost."

His eyes rested on the old man across from him. The man who had the answers to the questions he'd wanted to ask all his life. Fear and shame clouded his eyes.

"Was it my fault my mother crashed into that ravine? I've always wondered if I'd distracted her, if something I did caused her to miss that curve and go over the embankment.

"A few years ago, I drove back there, to the place we went over. How did I survive and she didn't? No seat belts, no car seats." He looked at Muley, his eyes begging for answers.

"Weren't your fault, boy. Your ma, well, she were unhappy with the university life. She didn't cotton to the parties and duties the professor's wife was supposed to help out with. Your ma was a good woman, but shy. She loved the reservation, her family, the Native American way.

"She took to sampling the wine to get through the days and nights. Billy, he tried to figure out a way to help her, but being a big-wig professor, and then a new author, kept him busy. Kept him traveling— alone." Muley didn't look at Oscar.

"Reckon it got to be too big a load for your ma. Billy said they had themselves an awful argument. Your ma wanted him to quit and move to the rez, teach school up there. Give back to their people." He chewed on his lip before he continued.

"Your pa said he refused. Told her he wasn't her people, he was Kickapoo. Said he was making a name for himself, for Native Americans. Said he stormed out the house and went to his office to work on his new book."

Silence filled the room. Then Muley let out a deep sigh, still not looking at the man across from him.

"Your pa said when he got home 'bout three in the morning, you and your ma was gone. Packed and gone, he said. Next thing he knew, the police were telling him you was in the hospital with broken bones, and your ma had passed on.

"He blamed hisself. Blamed his pride in being the only Native American teaching at the university, pride in having his book in print. Blamed hisself for the accident, he did. The police said she had a mite too much to drink and missed the curve, but your pa said it was his fault on account he drove her to drink.

"Next day he quit the university. Took his savings, money from his book, left his job, and moved to that there cabin he's been in all these years."

Oscar wiped tears from his cheeks. "Why couldn't he tell me that? Why couldn't he see I needed to know it wasn't my fault? Couldn't he see I needed him?

"I had a good life growing up with Mother Emma and Louise, but I wanted my father." Fists clenched on his knees, he growled, "I wanted my father. I wanted him to tell me it wasn't my fault my mother died. I wanted him to tell me he didn't blame me—he still loved me." And then he wept.

Muley waited, sipping his tea, silent in the storm of tears. When Oscar finally accepted the box of tissues offered, the old man patted the younger man's knee.

"Weren't the way men did things. Weren't supposed to cry, so we poked our hurts and our guilt and that there kinda feelings down so deep we lost sight of them.

"He didn't feel like he could be a good parent and raise you the way your ma wanted. So, I reckon, he left you with Emma so's he could honor your Ma's wishes."

"Thanks, Muley. Thank you for telling me—I know it had to be difficult for you, you being so close to my father—brothers. I just missed knowing him so much."

"Reckon your pa knew that. Reckon he knew you needed to hear the truth even if he couldn't speak it. Billy, he were a right good man, always helping out where he could. He used his money and his time to help folks in need, just couldn't see his way to helping you the way you needed to be helped. I'm sorry, boy."

The two men wiped their eyes and blew their noses. Oscar spoke first. "Well, I'm grateful to you for telling me. I forgave my father a long time ago. We made our peace. I'm grateful for being able to share the time we had, and I'll always cherish how he loved Molly, and now his great-grandson. Thanks, Muley."

He rose to leave. Muley pulled a spiral notebook from the top of the table. "Billy, he wanted you to have this. It's his story. Always thought he'd publish one more book before he died. When he knew it weren't gonna happen, he told me to make sure you got it after I told you about the accident. Be kind to his memory, boy. He were a good man. Not perfect, but dadblamed good."

Standing, he shook hands with Oscar and watched as Billy's son walked out to his car. Muley reckoned his step seemed a mite lighter.

SIXTY-ONE

Dan sat behind his desk, steaming cup of coffee and a plate holding a slab of Vicki's carrot cake sitting in front of him. Dipping his finger in the cream cheese icing, he let the sweetness melt on his tongue before sipping his coffee.

Deep in thought, he didn't notice the man at his door until he entered the office and plopped heavily into the chair across from him.

"Carter! It's great to see you. Let me pour you a cup of coffee. I'll bet Vicki has more carrot cake."

He noted the new lines of weariness that etched deep into his friend's face. Where once a near-constant smile bloomed, Carter's mouth drew down in bitter sadness.

"Come to drop off the checks I got from the folks who wanted me to re-open the café." He looked at Dan, his eyes dark pools of sorrow. "Can't seem to get the building planned. Can't seem to get any of it started. I figured I'd return the money and sell the lot. Let someone else put a café in there, if they have a mind to."

The sheriff studied his old friend. Shoulders drooped, face drawn with pain. The loss of Tina had taken the heart right out of him. Dan's own heart broke for him.

"Tell you what," he said, handing over a cup of coffee. "Hang onto those checks a bit longer. Never know what will happen, how things will change. Can't quit on us, Carter.

"Your loss is greater than we can comprehend, but I do know, if Baytree had succeeded in killing Molly, I don't know how I could go on." He dropped into silence thinking of the close call Molly and their unborn son had faced.

"Carter, going on without your wife, it's not going to be easy. Tina wouldn't want you to sorrow your life away, you know that. You two kept this town fed, and helped us come together as a community, with love and genuine joy in serving this town."

Carter blew on his coffee, took a sip and set the cup on the desk. Shaking his head, he said, "No reason to get up in the morning, Dan. No reason to open my eyes. Closed or open, I only see my wife, dying in my arms, helpless to stop it, and right there in front of our church. Why would a loving God let that happen?" His tears fell unchecked.

Vicki slipped in and set a plate with a piece of her cake next to his coffee. She laid her hand on Carter's shoulder, then left as silently as she'd entered.

Pulling a handkerchief from his back pocket, the grieving man mopped his face.

"It hurts, Dan. Our son has his own life up in St. Louis. It's just the dog and me at home. If it weren't for that mutt, I wouldn't get out of bed."

Nodding, Dan took a bite of cake, chewed, drank from his cup, and waited.

"If I did rebuild the café, who would help? I'd need help. Tina was always there--," his voice broke and he swiped at his eyes.

"God will provide what you need, Carter. I don't know why Tina had to go so young, but she loved and trusted God. We got to believe she is with Him.

"As far as getting help? Trust that it'll happen when the time is right. This town needs you, needs your café, and you need us. I can't promise the pain will go away, but it'll get easier to bear. Let your love for Tina, for Hilldale, touch the wounded folks all around you. We need you, Carter."

Dan drank from his mug and wiped his mouth with the back of his hand.

"Hilldale suffered and lost a lot at the hands of Baytree. But it's not farewell, my friend. It's a reason to rise up, to keep going forward. Only way to defeat darkness is with light. Even a tiny light will make a tremendous difference.

"Don't give up. I'll do what I can to help get you started. I know there's plenty of folks who'll step in, if they know you need them. Take the first step, Carter."

Silence filled the office as the two friends sipped their coffee and finished their cake. Carter set the empty plate on the desk.

"I could sell that woman's baked goods, they're so delicious." Looking up at Dan, his eyes held a spark of hope. "Guess maybe I might just see what I can do with a new place.

"Thanks, Dan. You've been a good friend, like a brother." He stood to go and Dan met him, embracing him for a moment.

"You let me know what you need, and I promise I'll get the word out to folks. You'll have more help than you can handle. You're doing the right thing, Carter. Won't be easy, but it's the right thing. Now, get out of here so I can get some work done."

Carter Neely hugged Dan hard. "Thanks, again, friend. I'll hold you to that promise."

SIXTY-TWO

"Papa?"

Carmen stared across the truck seat at Justin. Horror and shock widened her eyes. "Papa killed those men?" Her face drained of color and she traced the scars hash-marking her face. "Has he been arrested? I need to go back, help him with counsel."

Justin concentrated on the road, only stealing a quick glance at the agitated woman riding beside him. Traffic swirled around the pickup as he made his way southwest on I-44.

"He escaped. Hasn't been found, far as I know," he said, changing lanes to pass a slow-moving cattle truck. "I'm guessing he's headed to Mexico, maybe there by now. Changed vehicles at least once. He planned this out pretty well, Carmen."

Studying his profile, she saw no anger at her father's escape. "You going after him?"

"My guess is the process for extradition, if he's ever caught, will take a bit longer than usual. It's really in the Feds hands now.

"Dan has his hands full with the aftermath of the bombing, but he's cooperated with the U. S. Marshalls and FBI. All those lives lost, property damage—all must be documented and laid at the feet of the Baytree men. Long process, but eventually they'll find him. Bring him back to the states to stand trial.

"FBI might try their hand at going after your father, but my guess is they'll ask the U. S. Marshalls to chase him down."

"Conflict of interest for you?" Carmen asked, hope softening her voice.

"Not going to be a problem. Sent in my resignation last week. Dad thinks I should take the ranch on full time. Seeing as how you'll be there to help supervise, I took him up on his offer. Seems he has some private business somewhere south of the border—way south of the border."

Settling back, Carmen stared out her window watching the scenery fly by, letting her brain process all the news she'd just received.

Change. Life changed so quickly, and she wasn't sure she was prepared to meet the challenges all the changes would bring. Turning and looking at the man beside her, the man who'd risked everything to rescue her, to bring her to safety, she knew she was going to give it a darn good try.

"I love you, Justin Taylor," she said, smiling through the tears that trickled down her cheeks. "I'm grateful you didn't give up on me."

He reached over and took her hand. "Never," he said. "Never."

SIXTY-THREE

"**I**'m too dad-blamed old for this," Muley Burger whined to the young man sitting in the rocking chair across from him. The two men occupied the shabby porch at Muley's place in town. September sent a cool evening breeze that hinted of the change in seasons.

"I come to town to protect them ladies, and seeing as how I done bought Obed's place after he died, why, I figured life would be a bit more exciting, but this—," he snorted, "this last few months like to put me in my grave."

Gordie smiled at his dear friend. "Hadn't been for them women, you might be in that grave. Seems like they took right good care of you after you got hurt."

"You mean after that peckerwood Baytree nearly blowed me to bits. Don't mean to talk ill of the dead, but that there fella deserved what he got. Sorry if that's offending, but to my way of thinking, it's the truth."

Grunting, he gently tugged at Beauty's ears, scratched her head, and set his rocker into motion.

"Farm doing okay? I left you to all the work, but reckon you and Juanita 'bout run the place on your own already. That there wee one is going to be a big help, she gets a little growth on her. She's good with the critters, and Cootie took to her so much, he wouldn't stay in town with me. Moped and refused to eat 'til I took him back to the farm."

Gordie nodded. "She does have a way with living things. Got a gentle kindness about her I reckon come from God."

Looking at Muley, he asked, "You okay here in town? You can always move back to the farm. Be happy to have you."

The old man shook his head. "Got spoiled by them Harmon women. They cook and fuss over me. I do a few repairs and whatnot. Try to be useful and earn my meals.

"Reckon I'm fine here, boy. The farm is yours. It's all legal, and you know where the paperwork is. If I don't live too high off the hog here in town, might be a bit of pocket change for you, too. Since my Emily, you're the best thing ever happened to me, boy."

Muley looked at Gordie, and reaching across the empty space, took his hand. "You and your family give me a reason to keep going, and sure am grateful you all are in my life. Just want you to know that." Sniffing, he wiped his eyes and blew his nose.

"Strange, ain't it?" Gordie responded. "Seems like that scripture about God taking all the bad stuff and working it to our good, is true. After Ma was killed, I didn't know what was gonna happen to me.

All scarred and broken and backward as a stump. Who could want me, let alone love me?

"Then Sheriff Dan brought me to your farm, you took me in and loved me like your own. First, Uncle Billy, Sheriff Dan, Miss Molly—then my Juanita, and Little Wanda—why, I am blessed with family, Papa Muley. You all gave me a safe place to sorrow and grow through my hurt. You loved me when I was lost. So, reckon I'm the grateful one."

Looking at each other through their tears, they burst out laughing. Muley patted Beauty's head and rubbed her graying muzzle.

"Ain't God something? Don't reckon I understand His ways, but He sure gets the job done, don't He?"

One Year Later

SIXTY-FOUR

July sizzled its way into August. The heat dried out the Missouri clay and large cracks split the ground. Mud dauber wasps hung heavy in the late afternoon stillness.

Hot and muggy, the weather didn't keep the crowd away. Carter Neely stepped forward, and lifting an over-sized pair of scissors, he snipped through the bright purple ribbon tied across the entrance to Neely's Café.

Throwing open the door, cheers from the crowd rang out and Hilldale's folks streamed past him with congratulations. Carter looked toward heaven and smiled. Tina would have loved this—maybe was loving it even now.

Dan brought up the rear of the stampede. "Big crowd. Seeing as they just got done at the blessing of the new church, I figured you'd have a good turnout here. Got your hands full," he grinned, clapping his friend on the back. "Who's all helping inside?"

"Juanita, Gordie, Little Wanda, Mary, Wanda, umm, I think Muley's dispensing ice cream. Might be like putting a dog in charge of guarding the bones, eh?"

"Is Juanita staying on to cook?"

Carter nodded. "She's in charge of helping me mornings. Randy and Vicki are taking charge of evenings during the week. Their boys are helping out by doing the dishes and cleaning up. They seem to love it, and are doing a great job. Vicki's baked goods sell out as fast as we put them out. She baked triple batches of everything for this open house."

"Well, don't wear her out. We need her and Randy at the department. Hate to have to arrest you for some kinda trumped up charges just to get my own help back." Laughing, the men entered the happy noise of the town-folks celebrating another victory for the healing of Hilldale.

SIXTY-FIVE

Dan and Molly sat on their front porch and watched the sun dip low behind the courthouse. As the colors turned to brilliant oranges, reds, and yellow, arrows of light shot out setting the sky ablaze. For a moment, the world stood still as if listening for the close of day.

Billy crawled over to Dan and pulled himself up, grinning at the praise he received for his performance.

Molly laughed at her men. At the sound of her laughter, Billy turned, let go of Dan's knee and wobbled over to his mother, babbling a mile-a-minute.

Stunned, the two proud parents clapped and laughed as the little boy stood on his own two feet before plunking down on his diaper-padded bottom.

Closing his eyes, Dan breathed in the warm evening air. Just a year ago, Hilldale had suffered a terrible blow, but now, slowly, the small town was rising from the ashes of destruction, rebuilding its church, Neely's café, and the broken lives of the families that had lost loved ones.

The town pulled together, a community of love and caring, helping one another through the dark and lonely times. A year made a big difference, and Dan felt grateful that instead of falling apart and dying after the bombing, Hilldale had rallied and joined together to bring healing and new life to their town.

Those that lost loved ones that day, still sorrowed and missed them. But family and neighbors stepped in to comfort and care. The scriptures taught that we are to weep with those who weep, rejoice with those who rejoice, and over the past year, Dan had witnessed the town-folks do just that. Grateful. He was grateful.

SIXTY-SIX

In the tiny beach village of Puerto Escondido, Mexico, a man stands watching the sunset ease down on the ocean, splashing its vivid palate of colors in a path across the water.

Waves lap at his sandaled feet, and the silence of the evening is only broken by the calling of the birds heading for their roosts. Fruit bats flit through the evening sky, dark silhouettes against the sunset.

Clouds drift and shift patterns, and the man is sure the face of his daughter is drifting past, joyful in the evening light. Somehow, he knows she is well. The nightmares of the past are fading and she is happier, finding love again. He holds this belief close to his heart.

There is little regret except that he can't hug her, can't touch her scarred face with love. And he knows, one day there will be a knock on the door and he will be taken away. But for now, he is grateful that his daughter is free.

For this gift, he will gladly pay the price of only seeing her in the evening clouds, in his dreams, and in his prayers. Such is a father's love, to lay down his life for his child.

As darkness settles around him, he heads across the beach to a small casita resting among the trees. A lamp shines in the single window. He can hear the soft sounds of singing filtering from the open door, smell the mouth-watering aroma of his supper.

SIXTY-SEVEN

Loping along the canyon, the sun rose higher in the Texas sky, painting the landscape with the brilliant colors of dawn. Birds winged their way to nests full of hungry young. Cows called to their calves marking their location before going back to grazing.

Justin and Carmen reigned in their horses at the top of the hill, and in silence, watched the morning light sweep across the broad prairie, bringing it back to life for another day.

Watching as their cattle grazed, content with the grassy expanse rolling out before them; smiling at the frolicking calves, only taking time out to nudge and butt their mothers, drinking their fill before heading back to play; the two knew peace.

Carmen sighed. Justin leaned over and took her hand. "Well, Mrs. Taylor, how are you this morning? I must say you look stunning, as usual."

Pulling her hand free and smacking him lightly, Carmen smiled. "You are such a liar, but I love you anyway."

Her dark eyes searched his face. "It's been a good year for us, hasn't it, Justin? I'm so grateful for the ranch, for being with you. I love you, you know!"

Justin grinned. "Oh, I know. How could you not love me? I groom and saddle your horse for you every morning. I hired the best housekeeper-slash-cook in all of west Texas to set you free to do your volunteer work with the women and children's shelter."

"Okay! Enough, mister," Carmen laughed. Turning serious, she shifted in the saddle and reclaimed his hand.

"I am grateful for our life, Justin. This past year has had its ups and downs, but it's had healing, too. I'm grateful for your love, your patience, and care. Most of all, I'm grateful for being able to give back to those that need it. So many wounded and broken women and children. Some of the children have no home, no family."

Nodding, her husband looked out over the land. "We are blessed, my love. It's only right we share those blessings in any way we can. And you, Mrs. Taylor, you are doing wonderful work at the shelter.

"Speaking of sharing, have you heard any more on getting custody of Penelope? She seems pretty content to live with us at the ranch."

A broad smile lit Carmen's scarred face. "Today she will be in our permanent care. No one has come forward to claim her since she was left at the women's clinic as a newborn. Parental rights were terminated and we'll be able to file for adoption after a six-month waiting period. Are you up to having a two-year-old female running your life?"

Gathering up his reins, Justin laughed. "Can't see how it'll be much different than what I've got now?"

With that, he urged his horse forward. The morning breeze caught their laughter, lifting it as it soared to the heavens.

The End

Book Club Questions

1.   Do you identify with one or more of the characters? If so, how?

2. Have you ever been so angry or hurt you've allowed hate to rule? How did you resolve your feelings?

3. Discuss the moral issue of Manuel Fuentes taking the lives of the men who kidnapped and savaged his daughter. Was he right to do so? What do the scriptures say?

4. Discuss some ways Hilldale overcame the tragedies that beset it at the hands of James Baytree and his son.

5. Forgiving your enemies—do you think it's possible that it brings healing?

Acknowledgements

Russell, thank you for all you've given. Love triumphs.

Dee Solberg, daughter, massage therapist, writer, and brilliant editor—thanks for all the love, encouragement, and fearless editing. You are awesome. Your mother loves you!

To two of my sisters, Dorothy Rowden and Michele Gautsch, you ladies rock as beta readers, editors, and encouragers. Your emotional and spiritual support have blessed me through many trials. Love you!

Taylor and Justin, thanks for the loan of your names. The combo makes a great hero! Love you, grandkids.

Amy Bertling, you are a super business manager, friend, and prayer warrior. Your loving encouragement and editing skills have been invaluable. I love you like a daughter (Are you sure you're not my kid?).

Bianca Rascon and Perla Rascon, thank you for helping me keep my Spanish correct. Blessings!

A heartfelt thanks to Vicki Gares and all my beta readers. Your time and efforts on the behalf of my books are a constant blessing to me.

God is my anchor, and the anchor holds.

Hilldale Farewell

Author's Note: Over the past few years we've seen an escalation in hate: school shootings; children disappearing by the thousands being used for ill intent, often killed; blatant acts of terrorism all over this nation, and throughout the world—many in the name of vengeance/revenge.

   Hilldale Farewell grew into a book of renewal after vicious acts of terrorism on the small fictitious Missouri town of Hilldale, Missouri. As I pondered the story line, news reports of more shootings, more cars/trucks were run into innocent bystanders, churches invaded and worshipers destroyed, and my heart broke over the affect this took on the towns and cities, the trauma visited on those that lived and survived the onslaught of hate being visited on them.

   How to heal? How to get past the horrors? How to not only survive, but truly live again, with joy and purpose? How to leave fear behind and walk in the light once again?

   As I prayed for answers, pondering the sorrows and devastation, I could come up with only one answer: A change of heart. A change of heart, for myself, as a wounded follower of Jesus Christ, and for those also seeking answers.

   Only love can conquer hate. Sounds simple. It isn't. Believe me, I know. Sometimes it's a choice, a choice to love and forgive where love and forgiveness appear impossible. Forgiveness brings healing. Love grows, and renews, and brings the Light to cause the darkness to flee. How often I've wanted to retaliate, seek revenge, right the wrongs done to my loved ones, or to me! Then I'm reminded that revenge is not mine, not ours, but God's to deal with.

There will always be evil until our Savior comes and rescues this earth from the Prince of the Air. But if we, the people, can choose to promote God and His Son, Jesus; to love, not hate; forgive, not seek revenge; live in community, not isolationism; then I believe we can rise from the ashes of our lives with joy.

NOTE: DAN, originally published by Tate Publishing, is now re-published by Grand Circle Publishing, LLC under the title **STORM OVER HILLDALE** Book One of the Hilldale Missouri series.

Request for Reviews

Reviews are important to this author. If you would please take a few minutes to share on Amazon, BAM, or wherever you purchased it, it would be greatly appreciated. For contacting me, see the links below. Thank you!

Meet the Author

Pat Jaeger grew up in the Mid-West. The long cold winters made it perfect for reading books, playing guitar, and writing songs, poetry, short stories, and novels. Married with five grown children, a quiver full of grands and great-grands, she loves family get-togethers.

Drawing from her mom's stories of life growing up in rural Mid-Missouri, for the Hilldale series, as well as having lived there herself for nearly thirty years, Pat now lives and writes in Arizona with her husband and two rascally rescue dogs.

patjaegerspages.com
patjaegerspages@yahoo.com

Pat Jaeger

Books by Pat Jaeger

**Storm Over Hilldale - Hilldale Missouri Series,
Book 1**

**Home to Hilldale – Hilldale Missouri Series,
Book 2**

**Hilldale Farewell – Hilldale Missouri Series,
Book 3**

**Watch for Pat Jaeger's stand-alone Christian suspense
novel: BENT**

www.ingramcontent.com/pod-product-compliance
Lightning Source LLC
Chambersburg PA
CBHW061508050726
47593CB00002B/500

9 780099 820222 8